THE RUBY

Cass finds her friend Michael dead in his swimming pool, and while drowning appears at first to be the cause, evidence mounts that foul play was involved. The investigation brings the handsome Detective Inspector Noel Raven into Cass's life — and the connection between the two is literally electrifying. Cass's mother, a witch, warns her that she may be in deadly danger; only by working together can Cass and Noel hope to overcome the evil forces at work. Though Cass finds that her gemstones are also handy in a pinch . . .

Books by Fay Cunningham
in the Linford Romance Library:

SNOWBOUND
DECEPTION
LOVE OR MARRIAGE
DREAMING OF LOVE
FORGOTTEN

FAY CUNNINGHAM

THE RUBY
The Moonstones Trilogy

Complete and Unabridged

LINFORD
Leicester

First published in Great Britain in 2015

First Linford Edition
published 2016

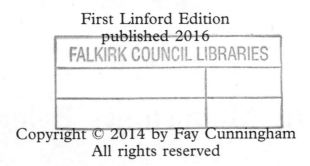

A catalogue record for this book is available
from the British Library.

ISBN 978–1–4448–2728–6

Published by
F. A. Thorpe (Publishing)
Anstey, Leicestershire

Set by Words & Graphics Ltd.
Anstey, Leicestershire
Printed and bound in Great Britain by
T. J. International Ltd., Padstow, Cornwall

This book is printed on acid-free paper

1

Cassandra Moon stood outside the house and wondered what was bothering her. The house looked beautiful, but something didn't feel right. It wasn't the house itself. The new building gleamed white in the afternoon sunshine; the freshly laid turf almost too green, the paths free from all the grime that normally accumulates on garden paths, the windows still factory-clean — everything as near perfect as it was possible to get. No, it wasn't the house. So why the scary feeling?

She walked up the path to the heavy wooden front door and pushed the bell, hearing the sound tinkle inside. After waiting patiently for several minutes she pushed the bell again. If Michael was expecting her, why wasn't he answering the door? She moved back a few steps to peer up at the house. Everything looked normal, but something had caused little goose bumps to break out on her bare arms.

The small leather bag hanging from her shoulder was starting to feel heavy, so she put a hand under the bag to support its weight and walked slowly round to the side of the house. The grass was damp in spite of the heat and a half-hidden sprinkler head almost tripped her up. The side gate, an imposing wrought-iron barrier with an electronic lock, was open — which was extremely odd. She must remind Michael how silly it was to have a state-of-the-art burglar alarm installed and then leave a gate open. Anyone could walk in.

She took a breath and eased the bag from her shoulder, wrapping the strap around her hand. Looking down, she saw she was now holding something that resembled a cosh. She eased the gate open and walked into the garden.

The first thing she saw was roses: roses every colour of the rainbow

climbing walls, tumbling from planters, and thickening the air with their heady scent. A couple of mature trees, deliberately left behind when the site was cleared, gave shade where it was needed, and she could see the unnatural blue of a new pool half-hidden down some steps. She wondered how often the pool would be used in the British climate, but today it was something to envy. The garden was designer-made, with nothing random and everything planned to within an inch of its life; but the effect was stunning. Concertina doors had been pushed hard back against the walls so the garden became part of the house, and from where she stood she could see into the living area. Two long white leather sofas dominated the room, a black-glass coffee table between them, and positioned on the far wall was the biggest flat-screen TV she had ever seen.

But no sign of Michael.

Cass walked into the house still feeling apprehensive. Michael had assured

her his new wife wouldn't be home until later, but technically she was trespassing. She called his name, listening to the echo as it bounced off the wooden floors and bare white walls. The floors needed rugs and the walls could do with some pictures, but the couple had only been home two days. Unwilling to go upstairs, and thinking Michael might have gone to sleep in the sun and not heard her, she walked slowly down the steps to the pool, expecting to see him sprawled in a lounger.

But he was face-down in the water at the shallow end of the pool, his arms and legs extended, his head completely submerged, his white hair moving like some strange sea anemone.

She had always imagined shock would galvanize her into action, but instead she froze, standing silent, her limbs rigid with fear. It seemed ages before she was able to move at all, and then all she could do was stumble to the side of the pool and fall to her knees beside her friend. She knew he was

dead, but she had to kick off her shoes and slide into the water just to be sure. Somehow she had to get him out of the pool. He was her friend, her mother's lover, and she had to rescue him from the cold blue water.

She couldn't lift him, so she pulled him to the steps; and once she had him partway out of the water, she managed to turn him over. He looked at her with his eyes wide open — eyes long dead. There was nothing else she could do, so she went back into the house, dripping water on the expensive parquet floor, and phoned for the police and an ambulance.

Waiting was difficult. She didn't want to leave him lying there alone, so she sat on a step just out of the water and rested his head in her lap. She stroked his wet hair and tried not to look at his sightless eyes, hoping someone would come soon. With nothing else to do, she looked for evidence of a fall, some reason for Michael to be dead, but there was no sign of anything out of place. A towel lay on the pale cream tiles and on top of the towel a pair of sunglasses glinted in the sun. A wine bottle and a single glass stood on a small table, the wineglass half-full, the bottle almost empty.

Cass frowned, her eyes moving back to the bottle and glass. Michael had been expecting her, and he knew she liked Chardonnay, so why only one glass? Perhaps he had come out to the pool earlier and been drinking for some time, intending to get another glass, and probably another bottle, after she arrived. If he had drunk more than half a bottle of wine it might explain why he'd fallen in.

Two paramedics, a man and a woman, came through the back gate at not quite a run. The man looked down at Michael's body lying in her arms. 'You found him in the water? Have you tried resuscitation?'

Cass shook her head. 'He was floating on the water at the shallow end, face-down. I dragged him to the steps and when I turned him over his eyes were open. I felt for a pulse in his neck, but there wasn't one, so I knew he was dead.'

The woman knelt down and carried out a brief examination. 'Been in the water for a little while, I would think. There wouldn't have been anything you could have done.'

Cass nodded. 'I know.' She let the woman support Michael's head and climbed out of the pool. She was wearing shorts, but the cuffs were wet and she was beginning to feel shivery.

'Doesn't look like a drowning,' the man said. He looked at Cass. 'Do you know if this person had a bad heart?' When she shook her head, he shrugged. 'We'd better leave it to the pathologist, then.'

It took them a few moments to remove Michael from the water. They tried to be gentle, and she was grateful for that. They were loading him onto a stretcher when the police arrived. Again, a man and a woman. Cass knew most of the Norton town police force, but she had never seen these two before. Detectives, she supposed, as they were wearing casual clothes: a motherly-looking woman wearing a white blouse and black skirt, dark curly hair pulled back off her face; the man in a T-shirt and jeans, trainers on his feet. When the woman saw the body on the stretcher her eyes flicked to Cass, but the man didn't even look at her. He was about six feet tall with broad shoulders and narrow hips. His black hair had been allowed to grow too long, giving him a slightly scruffy look, but it was his eyes that caught her attention — a steely grey that changed to silver in the sunlight.

He looked down at Michael without any sign of compassion and then took his time studying the area around the pool. Eventually his eyes settled on Cass. 'And you are — ?'

'Cassandra Moon. I got here about half an hour ago. The dead man is Michael Lansdale. I found him face-down in the water.'

'Noel Raven.' He didn't offer his

hand. 'Detective Inspector.'

'What happened to Detective Inspector Keely?'

'Promoted. He's the new DCI. I've taken his place.'

The paramedics covered Michael's body with a sheet and strapped him in to stop him rolling off the stretcher. He was a dead weight, and the woman found it difficult to move him, even though she only held his ankles.

'Drowning?' Raven asked.

The male paramedic shrugged. 'Not sure. If he was floating it means there wasn't enough water in his lungs to sink him to the bottom.'

Raven nodded. 'And not enough time for putrefaction to bring him up again. Could have been a heart attack, or he might have been falling-down drunk. Looks as if he's been at the wine. See if you can get a PM as soon as possible. Tell them it's urgent.' He took a mobile phone out of the pocket of his jeans and pushed buttons. Cass stood undecided, her wet shorts clinging to her thighs.

Could she go home, or was she supposed to stay and talk to the policeman before she left? She wanted to tell him it was unlikely Michael had been drunk. Apart from the occasional glass of wine, he drank very little.

The commotion began near the gate, with raised voices, and then a scream that sounded like an animal in pain. Cass leaped to her feet, only to be stopped by an arm thrust out in front of her. 'Stay here,' Raven commanded.

He started away from her at a run, but not quickly enough to stop the wild-eyed woman rushing down the steps towards the pool. Raven caught her in mid-flight with an arm round her waist. 'Whoa, wait just a minute.' She was followed by a very contrite-looking uniformed police officer. 'I thought I told you not to let anyone in,' Raven said mildly, still holding the frantic woman in his arms.

'Sorry, sir. She drove up and saw the ambulance and asked what was going on.'

'And you told her.' He tried to lead the woman to a chair, but she broke away from him and dropped to her knees beside the stretcher. She pulled back the sheet and Cass was pleased to see one of the paramedics had closed Michael's eyes.

'Michael?' The woman's hand reached out to touch his face, but she quickly drew it back. 'What's wrong with him? What have you done to him?'

This must be Michael's new wife, Cass realised. The woman he was so proud of. The woman he wanted to introduce to all his friends. She fished in the back of her mind for a name. Debbie. Debbie Lansdale, married for a little while to Michael Lansdale, and now a widow. Cass walked over to the distraught woman and squatted down beside her.

'Debbie, let me take you inside the house. They have to take Michael away now.'

But the detective was there before Cass had time to stand up again. 'Officer

Stubbs will take you inside, Mrs Lansdale. I'll come and talk to you in a little while.'

Cass climbed shakily to her feet, really cold now in spite of the sun. She wrapped her arms around her body, watching them take Michael away. 'I should go home.'

'Yes.' Raven looked her up and down. 'You're wet and you need to change your clothes.' As she started to walk away he put a hand on her arm. 'Before you go, I need to ask about your relationship with Lansdale and your reason for being here.'

'I was doing some work for him, but he's also a friend.'

'So are you here on business, or was it purely pleasure this time?'

Did he think they were having an affair? 'Business,' she told him coolly. 'I haven't seen Michael for a while — he'd been in Spain for several years — but we kept in touch by phone or email.' She was cold and wet and feeling decidedly wobbly. She didn't want to answer his questions. 'I work mostly from home. I have a workshop attached to the house.'

'Good. I'll come round and take a statement from you tomorrow. You can give me the details then.'

She shook her head. 'I'd rather you didn't come to my house. I live with my . . . '

'Sorry. That wasn't a request.'

'It will be easier if I come to the police station.'

'Like I said before, Miss Moon, I wasn't giving you a choice. I'll be round to see you tomorrow morning at about ten o'clock.'

She was too tired to argue with this man. 'Very well.' She picked up the little bag from the table and slipped the strap over her shoulder. It felt even heavier than before. She looked at Raven in disbelief when he held out his hand.

'What's in the bag? May I have a look, please?'

'Certainly.' She tossed the bag to

him, perversely pleased when he almost dropped it.

'Bloody hell! What have you got in here?'

'Stones.'

He undid the flap and peered inside cautiously as if he was expecting a snake or, at the very least, a gun.

'Please be careful,' she said, as he shook the little velvet bags out and put them on the glass top of the table. 'There's an expensive mix of stones in there. And no, in answer to your next question, I'm not a burglar, I'm a jeweller.' She put a hand in her pocket and handed him a card. 'My jewellery business is called Moonstones.'

He opened one of the bags and tipped the three small stones into the palm of his hand. He had chosen well.

'Rubies,' she said.

He stared at the stones. 'They don't look like rubies.'

'They're uncut. I think they're even more beautiful in their natural state. I have diamonds as well, but they're not

14

as pretty as the rubies. In a polished but uncut state, the coloured stones are the prettiest.' She chose a bag from the table. 'See, these are polished tiger's eyes. In the sunlight they look as if they're filled with bands of gold.'

He looked up at her and smiled, and for a fleeting moment she saw a different man. 'You obviously enjoy your work.'

'Yes, I do. Michael wanted some jewellery designed for his wife without her knowing, so he asked me to bring some gemstones for him to see before his wife got back from London.' Cass packed the stones back into their respective bags and looked over at the house. 'Should I go and talk to Mrs Lansdale, do you think? She doesn't know anyone here in Norton. They only arrived back from Spain yesterday.'

'I'll send for a FLO — a family liaison officer. If necessary she'll stay the night with Mrs Lansdale. If a bereavement counsellor is needed, we can arrange that later.'

Cass stifled a yawn. She was exhausted, and before she arrived home she had to find the right way to tell her mother Michael was dead.

Noel Raven dismissed her with a wave of his hand. 'Go home, Miss Moon. I'll see you tomorrow.'

She drove home slowly. She had been looking forward to seeing Michael again. He'd been away for almost five years, with only the occasional visit back to England, and she'd been excited about meeting his new wife — but not like this. The woman had looked completely bewildered. She had only been married to Michael a few weeks and now he was dead. If the cause of death proved to be a heart attack, the poor woman would forever blame herself for not being there. As it was, Cass wished she'd arrived earlier. She might have been in time to help him.

When she got home her mother was in the kitchen. Dora Moon was a small woman with silver hair long enough to curl on her shoulders and pretty blue eyes. She was wearing a caftan in jungle green, her feet bare. She greeted her daughter with a sad little smile.

'He's dead, isn't he?'

Cass didn't bother to ask how her mother already knew. She was used to Dora Moon knowing every event that happened in the town well in advance of everyone else. Dora sold recipes on the Internet and spent most of her time on Facebook or Twitter or some other chat-room. Local news travelled like an express train. Cass nodded, taking the mug of tea her mother handed her.

'Yes, he's dead. He drowned in his swimming pool. They think he had a heart attack.' She touched her still-damp shorts. 'I need to go up and change.'

'He didn't drown,' Dora said. 'He was murdered.'

Cass sighed. 'I suppose technically he didn't drown, because it looks as if he was dead before he fell in, but he wasn't murdered. Who would want to murder Michael?'

'I don't know, but somebody did. And don't make a face. The sugar in your tea is good for shock.'

'A police detective is coming here tomorrow to take a statement. Please don't mention murder to him.'

Dora picked up Cass's mug and tipped the tea down the sink. 'I hope he's clever enough to find out who killed Michael.'

2

Noel Raven pushed away the last of the files on his desk. He wouldn't have taken the job if he'd known how much paperwork it entailed. How was he supposed to solve any cases if he had to spend hours on unimportant documentation?

Detective Sergeant Brenda Stubbs popped her head round the door. She was in her early fifties, married, with two teenage children and one of his best detectives. 'It's going to be a few days before we get a tox report back, even though I told them it's urgent.'

'Damn! I need to know how the man died. Did he fall, or was he pushed? When's the PM?'

'Again, a day or two. They've got two hospital litigation cases to deal with.'

'More important than my unexplained death?'

''Fraid so.'

Noel got to his feet. 'Tell the lab to give me anything that shows up in the blood or urine. If alcohol is present, I want to know how much. The body was fresh so they should be able to find something. I need to know how Michael Lansdale died.'

Brenda made a note on her pad. 'I'll do my best. What makes you think he didn't just fall in the pool? Heart attack or something?'

'The paramedic at the scene thought he must have been dead before he hit the water because he was floating. Yeah, it could have been a heart attack or a stroke, but it must have been damned quick.'

'What do you want me to do?'

'Try and hurry things up, otherwise this is going to go down as accidental death. The family will bury him, and we'll never find out what really happened.' Noel stared into space. 'No point in doing a door-to-door. There are no neighbours to speak of and it will just stir up speculation. We'll keep this as a natural death until we know otherwise. See if you can get me a verification of the time Mrs Lansdale's train arrived from London.' He picked up a single sheet of paper from his desk. 'Kevin didn't get much out of her before the doctor dosed her up. I'll give her a call tomorrow when she's had a night's sleep and calmed down a bit.' He looked at his watch. 'I'm going to call on Cassandra Moon later this morning and get a statement from her. Know anything about her?' He had discovered Brenda was a good source of local information. She'd lived in Mickford all her life, was well liked, and knew a lot of the local inhabitants personally. Now she grinned at him.

'A pretty redhead with blue eyes. Still under thirty and not married or engaged. She lives with her mother and makes beautiful, original jewellery I wish I could afford.' The grin widened. 'Watch your back when you visit because her mother's a witch.'

Noel put the piece of paper back on his desk. 'What sort of witch? Just a nasty piece of work, or someone who's likely to put a spell on me?'

'I don't want to spoil the surprise, but I should carry a clove of garlic and a cross if I were you.'

'As long as she doesn't do back-street abortions, or grow marijuana in the garage, she's entitled to follow any profession she chooses, and I think witchcraft is one of the oldest — before prostitution even.' He consulted a handwritten list. 'See if you can find out why Mrs Lansdale went to London and get verification of her visit. She told Kevin she had an appointment, but not with whom. If she was actually in the city and can prove it, I can cross her off my list of suspects.' He glanced down at the paper in his hand. 'It's not a long list because I only have two suspects at the moment, Cassandra Moon and Deborah Lansdale, but I'm sure it will get longer. While we're waiting for the tox screen get someone to check them both out. I need a case file on each of them and it needs to be thorough.'

As soon as Brenda left the room he turned on his computer and Googled Cassandra Moon. There were a dozen or so women with that name, mostly oriental, but she was easy to spot. She had her own web page with pictures of her jewellery. Beautiful classic pieces using a variety of gemstones, pearls and amber. Most of her work was made to order and she didn't sell abroad. Yesterday she had been wet, cold and frightened, probably not at her best, but there had been something about her that told him she wasn't a suspect, and that was a dangerous assumption for someone in his profession. All he could remember clearly was a long fall of copper hair, and lavender eyes. The way her damp skirt clung to her legs was something he was still trying to forget.

Pandora Moon, he discovered, was a fictional character in a TV series, but the lady he was looking for was prominent on Facebook and had an incredible number of 'friends'. She seemed to have a natural remedy for every ailment on the planet and he now knew exactly where to go if he suddenly sprouted warts between his toes. Pandora gave advice on everything from childbirth to divorce and sold recipes for herbal remedies online. On her Twitter page she mentioned that she couldn't leave the house — and Noel wondered why.

He opened a blank page on Word and started a profile for everyone connected with Lansdale's death, however remote that connection was. By the end of the week he hoped to have a nice thick file. He had a gut feeling this was going to turn into a murder investigation, and he wanted to get a head start. But at the moment all he had was his gut feeling and the paramedic's report. Lansdale hadn't swallowed or inhaled enough water to take him to the bottom of the pool, and Noel had noticed grazes on the man's bare knees and shins as though he'd crawled or been dragged across the tiles surrounding the pool. He cursed the fact that he was sitting here playing with a computer when he needed some positive evidence. He looked at his watch and stood up. It was time to visit Cassandra Moon and her interesting mother.

He walked through the outer room and waved a hand at his team, but before he could open the door, Brenda handed him a small packet.

'Put that in your pocket. You might need it.'

Noel looked at the tiny white packet lying on his palm. 'Salt?'

'It's supposed to ward off evil spirits,' she said with a grin. 'Dora Moon is a force to be reckoned with. You'll need all the help you can get.'

'Don't worry. If I get cornered by an evil spirit, I turn into my namesake bird and get the hell out.' He dropped the packet into his pocket. 'But thanks for the concern.'

He had trouble finding the house. The sat nav didn't seem to have a clue and the house didn't have a number, just a name. He should have known, he thought, as he backtracked and saw the sign. The house was called Abracadabra. One of the oldest and most potent incantations of all time.

Deciding not to drive right up to the house in case he couldn't turn round, he parked on the grass verge and walked up a short, leafy track that led to a front door the colour of fresh blood. He wondered why that particular association had popped into his head, and smiled when he realised his fingers had closed round the packet in his pocket.

The paint on the door looked bright red from a distance, but when he got closer all he could see was dry, peeling paint, the colour dulled by wind and rain. There was no bell, only a heavy black iron knocker in the shape of a bird. A raven? Now he really was getting fanciful.

Before he could lift the knocker, the door opened.

She was taller than he remembered, her bright hair falling in soft curls past smooth tanned shoulders. He had been right about her eyes; they were more lavender than blue, fringed with lashes several shades darker than her hair.

Women didn't usually rattle him, but it took him a moment to get his breath; and then all he could manage was a feeble, 'Hi.'

She held the door wide and turned away from him. 'You'd better come in.'

By now he should be used to the fact that he wasn't everyone's most welcome visitor, but it still surprised him sometimes. After all, he had given her his most charming smile.

The hallway was unusually light. From outside the house had looked dark and gloomy, but a large gold-framed mirror bounced the morning sunlight off pale cream walls and a bowl of blue flowers filled the air with a pleasant scent. Cassandra was about to open a door off the hall when a small fairy-like woman appeared from the

27

back of the house, wiping her hands on a tea towel.

'Oh, don't take the poor man in there, Cassie; you know we keep that room for people we don't like. Come into the kitchen, Noel. I've just made a pot of tea.'

He tried not to show his surprise at the use of his first name. Dora Moon couldn't have been much over five feet tall. Soft white hair curled round her small pixie face and her feet were bare, each toenail painted a different colour. She didn't look like a witch — just interesting.

This time his smile was more relaxed. 'Thank you, Mrs Moon. I'd love a cup of tea.'

'Dora, please, otherwise I shall have to call you Mr Raven — and we don't want to get all formal, do we? Mind you, Raven is a good name. Dark, and very masculine.' She paused for a moment as if she had forgotten what she was talking about. 'Oh yes, I've made biscuits, too. Chocolate chip cookies. They'll spoil your lunch, but who cares.'

He heard Cassandra sigh as he followed her mother into the kitchen, and he gave her a curious look. Was this the reason she'd wanted to make her statement at the police station? He wondered for a moment if she were ashamed of her mother, but she looked more resigned than embarrassed.

'Do you know how Michael died?' she asked, as he sat down at the kitchen table and started on the biscuits Dora put in front of him. 'The paramedic said something about Michael not drowning.'

'We're still waiting for the post-mortem results.' He dunked his biscuit in his tea. It was really good. 'But it looks as if Lansdale was dead before he went into the water.'

'He was murdered,' Dora said matter-of-factly.

Noel looked at the woman curiously. 'What makes you say that, Mrs Moon?'

'I said to call me Dora. Mrs Moon makes me feel old. I told Cassie

Michael was murdered. I saw him in the water — and he wasn't alone. There was someone else at the house before Cassie got there.'

He was more curious than sceptical. 'Why do you think Lansdale was murdered?

Dora smiled at him, showing small white teeth. 'Because I'm a witch and I see things.'

He didn't smile back. Instead, he looked across the table at Cassandra. 'I hope it wasn't murder, Dora, because that would make your daughter the prime suspect.'

'Yes, it would, wouldn't it? So it's a good job she didn't do it.' Dora picked up the plate and held it out to him. 'Have another biscuit, Noel.'

Once he'd finished his tea and biscuits he got out his notebook and took Cassandra Moon's statement. She went through her visit one step at a time, sticking strictly to the facts.

'You moved the body.'

'I didn't know he was dead until I got in the water,' she said defensively. 'I couldn't just leave him there. He might still have been alive. He was lying face-down, but when I turned him over I knew straight away he was dead.'

'How did you know that?'

Cassandra took a breath and he could see her reliving the moment. 'I knew he was dead because his eyes were wide open and he didn't have a pulse.' She looked at him and he could see worry in her amethyst eyes. 'He was dead, wasn't he?'

Noel nodded, glad he could put her mind at rest. 'Yes. They haven't done a full post-mortem yet, but it looks as if he'd been in the water about an hour before you found him. It's difficult to be accurate because it was a very hot day and the pool water was quite warm.' He looked at her thoughtfully. 'Would Mr Lansdale normally conduct a business meeting in his swim shorts?'

Dora interrupted with a laugh. 'It wasn't a business meeting. Cassie's known Michael all her life. He's like a father to her.'

'It would have been an informal chat and a drink by the pool,' Cassandra said. 'I wanted him to choose some stones for a necklace. A present for his wife. It's her birthday in a few weeks' time.'

'What will you do about the necklace now?'

'I don't know.' She frowned, making little creases in her smooth forehead. 'I suppose I could phone her and tell her Michael had a present planned for her birthday, but I don't want to upset her.'

Noel picked up Cassandra's signed statement and got to his feet. 'You should call her. She might be in need of a friend right now.'

★   ★   ★

Dora saw him out and came back into the kitchen with a big smile on her face. 'Nice. Tall, dark, and good-looking. You'll have to see more of him.'

'No thank you, Mother. He's a policeman.'

Dora shrugged. 'You may not have a choice, Cassie.'

That was the second time Cass had been told she didn't have a choice. Ignoring her mother, she went out the back to her studio. The place had once been a garage, but as there was plenty of parking in front of the house the walls had been boarded over and a new floor put down. The once up-and-over door was now a floor-to-ceiling window, and a workbench had been built beneath the window. A wall of shelves held the various tools she needed to make her jewellery. She had added pictures, a small sofa, a coffee machine, and a CD player. Her computer sat on a desk in the corner.

She put the velvet bags in the wall safe and made sure the drawers of semi-precious stones were securely locked. This was her favourite place. For many reasons it would have been stupid to live away from home, but occasionally she needed her own space, and this was it. She had her own bedroom in the house, complete with en-suite bathroom, but she shared the living room and kitchen with her mother, and sometimes her mother could be a trifle tiring.

She felt restless. She wanted to get on with Michael's necklace, but whether she went ahead was going to be up to his new wife. She took a shaky breath, remembering Deborah Lansdale was now a widow.

She picked up the phone on the off-chance her friend could make lunch in town. Liz was a nurse at the local hospital and worked a mix of nights and days. The phone rang for several seconds, and Cass had been about to hang up when Liz answered.

'Hi, Cass — and before you ask, no, you didn't wake me. I've got two whole days off, then back on nights. I heard about Michael. It was on the local news. I'm so sorry.'

'I found him in their new pool when I got to the house. At the moment I can't seem to get my head round the fact that he's dead. Dora's talking her usual rubbish, so she's not much help, but I think it hit her harder than she's letting on. Can you meet me for lunch? I promise I won't be miserable.'

'You have a perfect right to be miserable. I'll see you in twenty. Usual place.'

They always met at a pub in the High Street where parking was free as long as you ate something. Cass squeezed her small car into one of the last few parking spaces and walked in through the back entrance. Liz was easy to spot with her black, spiky hair. She had the beautiful latte-coloured skin that comes from mixed-race parents, and a smile white enough and bright enough to light up a room. She had already found a table in the courtyard garden and once they each had a glass of Chardonnay in front of them, Liz asked Cass about Michael. 'I only met him a couple of times. But he seemed like a lovely man.'

'He was.' She spent a few minutes running through the sequence of events at Michael's house. 'The paramedic seemed to think Michael was dead before he fell in the pool. Something to do with the fact that if he was floating on top of the water he didn't actually drown.'

'He might have had a heart attack or a stroke while he was standing near the edge of the pool. If his heart stopped before he fell in he wouldn't have any water in his lungs.'

Cass took a sip of her wine. 'My mother says he was murdered.'

Liz smiled. 'How is Dora? Has her cold gone yet?'

'Yes, but the smell of the herbs and things she boiled up hasn't. I told her paracetamol would work just as well, but no, she had to make this disgusting concoction and then drink it. It's a wonder it didn't poison her.'

'It evidently cured her cold.'

Cass snorted. 'It was a forty-eight-hour thing. It would have gone in a couple of days. I told her not to say anything to the policeman, but you know she can't keep her mouth shut.

When he came round to the house she told him Michael had been murdered. He wasn't impressed. He said that would make me the prime suspect.'

'What policeman?'

'Keely's replacement. Tall, dark, and arrogant. Not a bit like Keely.'

Liz put her elbows on the table and rested her chin in the palms of her hands. She smiled across the table at Cass. 'Describe him exactly and in detail. Tall and dark sounds good, but would it be possible to replace the word 'arrogant' with 'handsome'? If he's ugly and arrogant, I don't want to know.'

'He's a bit too casual-looking for a policeman, but he's a detective, so I suppose he can dress how he pleases. His hair is too long, practically onto his shoulders, and he dunks his biscuits in his tea. I wouldn't be surprised if he has several other nasty habits as well. He needed a shave when I first met him, so he had dark stubble on his face, and he has these really weird eyes. A sort of pale silvery grey that darkens like a thundercloud when he gets annoyed.'

'Thank you. That was a very graphic description.' Liz sighed. 'Designer stubble as well. He sounds just perfect.' She sat back and took a sip of wine. 'Come to think of it, you seem to have spent an awfully long time looking into his eyes. When are you seeing him again?'

'Hopefully never. I don't believe Michael was drunk, and if he thought he was having a heart attack he would've gone indoors and phoned for help.'

Liz shook her head. 'An embolism can be really sudden and take someone completely by surprise. He might have been walking down the steps when he was taken ill, and dead before he hit the water. It can be that quick.'

They stopped talking while their sandwiches were put on the table. Liz stared at her plate. 'I chose an egg and cress sandwich because that was the least fattening, but I've got a plate full of crisps as well. What am I supposed to do — leave them?'

Cass picked one up. 'No problem. I'll

eat them for you.' She popped the crisp in her mouth. 'I want your advice, Liz. What do I do about the pendant necklace Michael ordered? He sent me a cheque for a thousand pounds, so I'm going to have to speak to his wife at some point. I don't want to sound as if I'm trying to push her into buying something from me, but just handing the cheque back seems rude.'

Liz picked up a crisp, looked at it sadly and put it back on the plate. 'I think you're making too much of it. Just ask her on the phone if she wants you to finish the necklace; if not, return the cheque. What's the problem?'

Cass shifted uncomfortably on her chair. 'I thought I was going to like her right away, the way Michael spoke about her, but I'm not sure I did.'

'You told me you only saw the woman for a matter of seconds. You can't make a decision like that until you've had a chance to talk to her properly. She'd just walked in on a dead husband. I doubt she was at her best.'

'No, you're right, first impressions are often wrong. Michael was looking forward to introducing us. He told me we'd get along really well.'

Liz pushed her plate away with a little sigh. 'And I'm sure you will — when you get a chance to know her better.'

'So you think I should call her?'

'Yes.' Liz gazed longingly at her plate. 'Cass, if you love me, please eat the rest of those crisps.'

Cass covered the remaining crisps with a napkin. 'I don't want them. I know when to stop.' She laughed at her friend's muttered comment. 'Thanks for meeting me, Liz. I'm feeling all over the place at the moment, but you cheered me up no end.' As they walked back to their cars, she said, 'I need to know how Michael died. I keep thinking if I'd got there sooner he wouldn't be dead.' She knew her thoughts were irrational — they often were — but the niggle of doubt remained.

'It wasn't your fault, Cass,' Liz told her. 'Once they've done the post-mortem, I'll see if I can get a look at the report. That should tell us something.'

Cass thanked her friend and drove home. She parked the car and went straight into her studio, bypassing the house. The studio was the one place her mother would never enter without permission. She kicked off her shoes and threw herself onto the settee. Pushing the button on the CD player gave her Jamie Cullum. Muting the sound, she allowed the piano to tinkle in the background. She could cope with Michael's death. People die all the time, sometimes quietly and sometimes with a fanfare of trumpets — that she could accept. But this was all wrong.

She unlocked the safe and took out the bags of stones she had taken for Michael to look at. Walking over to her workstation, she tipped the gemstones onto the bench. What would Michael have chosen? She had suggested a birthstone and Michael had told her

Debbie's birthday was mid-July, which made her birthstone a ruby. A well-cut ruby in a true red can cost more than a diamond, so she was pleased Michael thought Debbie would like the stone in its uncut form. Working with stones costing several thousand pounds each made her very nervous.

She pushed the stones on the bench around with the tip of her finger. Maybe a ruby tucked into an intricate twist of gold for the centrepiece, with pearls on either side. The ruby stands for eternal love, which had seemed appropriate at the time.

She was already beginning to visualise the necklace in her head. She picked up a pad and pencil to jot down her ideas and, by the time she finished, she had a sketch for a piece of jewellery that would be unique as well as beautiful. Pleased with herself, she locked the stones away again and went to find her mother.

Tomorrow she would phone Debbie Lansdale.

3

For some reason the house looked even larger second time around. Cass paused on the front path as she had before and stood, just looking. Nothing had really changed. The windows were a shade darker than she remembered, the front door even more imposing — but the grass, so green on her first visit, seemed to have lost some of its vigour. Perhaps the sprinklers were switched off.

Once again the leather bag was slung over her shoulder, the same stones snug in their velvet pouches, the sense of déjà vu almost overpowering.

Her phone call to Debbie Lansdale the evening before had been brief. Michael's wife had said she would be delighted to see Cass. Michael had talked a lot about his friend and Debbie was looking forward to meeting her. Cass had listened closely for any hint of animosity, but there was none. The woman just sounded friendly.

Now here she was.

Before she pushed the bell she tried to remember what Michael's wife looked like. Their eyes had met very briefly over his dead body, and the images in her head were distorted. Whether the woman was tall or short, she had no idea. She did remember pale skin, light hair and bright blue eyes, but not much else. To find out, all she had to do was ring the doorbell. Why was that proving so hard?

The woman who answered the door was taller than Cass had remembered, but the eyes were the same, the blue still far too intense for the pale skin, so probably contacts. Soft blond hair curled gently on Debbie Lansdale's bare shoulders, and a tentative smile hovered round her mouth as if she wasn't sure smiling was appropriate. She was wearing a bright red top and white cut-off jeans, with strappy sandals on her bare feet. Cass felt positively underdressed in denim shorts and a white T-shirt.

She held out her hand. 'Cassandra Moon. I wish we could have met in better circumstances. Michael was like a father to me.' She wanted to get that in quickly to avoid any confusion. At one time she had been sure Michael *was* her father. When she was a child he was a regular visitor, and she had no other candidates to choose from.

'Please come in.' Debbie led the way into the lounge area. She lifted her arm to take in the large room and then let it drop again. 'There was so much I planned to do. Michael had already arranged for a designer to come in, but the place is too stark for me. Too empty.' She brushed a hand across her face. 'I was planning on making it a home.'

'You still can. Unless you intend to go back to Spain.'

'Oh, I won't do that.' The woman sounded shocked. 'Did you think I might want to?'

'I suppose all your friends are there. You'd been living abroad before you met Michael, hadn't you?'

'Only about a year. I moved out there after my divorce. I didn't think I would ever meet anyone else. Not someone I could spend the rest of my life with.' She tried a little smile, her eyes bright with tears. 'Then Michael came along.'

Cass decided she had better change the subject before she started crying as well. 'I've brought the stones with me, in case you want to have a look, but there's no obligation. I've made out a cheque for the money in case you want to cancel the order.'

'No. This was a present from Michael, even though he's not able to give it to me himself. I couldn't possibly return it. Please sit down.'

Cass sat down on the white sofa and spread a small velvet cloth on the glass-topped coffee table. She shook the rubies out of their bag. 'Your birthstone is a ruby. The rubies are uncut, but I can get other stones in practically any colour you want.'

'You mentioned my birthstone on the phone. Had Michael already chosen the stones?'

'Michael just made a few suggestions. He liked the idea of rubies and pearls, so I'd already made a rough design . . . '

Debbie poked at the rubies with her finger. 'They don't look like rubies, do they?'

Cass was used to this reaction. She had seen it many times before. At a quick glance the uncut stones looked dull and lifeless, but once they were polished and set in gold or some other precious metal, they would take on a life of their own. Rubies had a mystic quality when worn by the right person.

'Sometimes a mix of stones can look fabulous.' She unrolled her design and laid it out on the table. 'I've done some of the work already and it should look good when it's finished. The centrepiece is a ruby in a flower of gold wire with pearls amongst the leaves on each side. I can do earrings to match if you like, using the two smaller rubies and more pearls.' She waited, but Debbie was still studying her design.

'Could you use diamonds instead of pearls, just to give the whole thing a bit of a sparkle?'

'I can do that, but uncut diamonds don't look like much. Rubies and pearls would be a perfect birthday necklace.'

'Yes, of course.' Debbie shook her head. 'What do I know? You're the expert. Whatever you think Michael would have chosen will be wonderful.'

She persuaded Cass to stay for a glass of Chablis, taking the wine from a cooler and glasses from a display cabinet, and then confided she was dreading the arrival of Michael's two children.

'They'll hate me, I know they will. They already think I'm a gold-digger, just after their father's money. His son emailed Michael all the time, telling him not to be a stupid old fool.' She reached into her bag and pulled out a tissue. 'I would have made Michael a good wife, and it would be nice to think I had his children's support, but I don't expect I'll get it.'

'Don't judge them before you've met them,' Cass said, remembering her mother's words. 'They may take you by surprise.'

'Oh, I'm sure they will,' Debbie Lansdale sniffed into her tissue. 'The girl was OK about Michael getting married again — she was prepared to withhold judgement until she met me; but the boy — he's older than me, so he's hardly a boy — he wasn't having any of it. He really upset Michael on a couple of occasions. I think he only gets in touch when he needs money for something.'

Cassandra knew Michael's children very well; when she was small she had spent a lot of time with them. Colin could be awkward at times, but he wasn't nearly as bad as Debbie made out. 'If you need any help organising things,' she said awkwardly, 'please let me know.' Someone was going to have to arrange the funeral once the body was released, and she really didn't want to get involved with that, but thankfully Debbie changed the subject.

'Maybe, when you've done a little work on the necklace, you could bring it round so I can get an idea of what it's going to look like. To be honest, I don't know anyone here, and I'm hoping to make some friends eventually.' She smiled wistfully. 'Michael was going to organise a few dinner parties to introduce me to everyone. This is all very different from what I'm used to.'

Cass got to her feet. 'I'll come and see you again in a few days. And thank you for the wine.' She packed up her stones and left Debbie alone in the big house. She should be feeling sorry for the woman and couldn't understand why she wasn't. She had been really happy and excited when Michael phoned to tell her he was getting married again. He had talked about Debbie a lot in his emails to her and her mother, and Cass had formed a picture in her head. Debbie seemed a really nice woman, but for some reason she wasn't at all what Cass had expected.

She was halfway home when her mobile phone started to buzz on the passenger seat next to her. There was nowhere to pull over, so she ignored it, but a few seconds later it started up again. Thinking it might be her mother, she pulled into an empty driveway and picked up the phone.

'Miss Moon?'

She recognised the voice. 'Inspector Raven, what can I do for you?'

'I need to see you.'

Because she couldn't think of anything to say, she didn't say anything.

'I'm not asking you out on a date, Miss Moon.' The exasperation was painfully evident in his tone. 'I need to speak with you. A couple of queries on your statement.'

Someone hooted behind her. 'I'm sitting in someone's driveway.' She put her car in reverse and waited for the other car to move out of her way. 'I don't understand. I told you everything when you came to the house.'

'Just a few things I need to get clear in my head. What *is* that noise?'

'Someone banging on my car window. Wait a moment . . . ' She rolled down her window. 'What is the matter with you?' she shouted at the elderly man who was glaring at her. 'I'm trying to get out of your way, but I can't move until you get out of mine.' She shot the window back up before he could hit her, which he looked as if he might. Looking in her rear-view mirror, she watched him get back into his car and inch out onto the busy road. 'I believe it's illegal to talk on the phone while I'm driving, so I'll have to call you back.'

She cut Raven off and managed to reverse out of the man's driveway, continuing down the road for several hundred yards before she found another place to stop. Checking the last caller on her mobile, she phoned him back. 'Sorry about that.'

'Your mother said you were visiting Deborah Lansdale but you'd already left. I just need a few minutes of your time.'

Cass had heard that before. 'Do you want me to come to the station?'

'No, I'm in town and I need a coffee. Meet me in Costa. The one in the high street.'

'OK, but I'll have to . . . park somewhere,' she said to a dead phone.

She found a place for her car in the multi-storey, having almost decided to park on double-yellows — she was on police business, after all. She found him sitting in a corner of the busy shop, two lattes and a pile of papers in front of him.

'I didn't do it,' she said, slipping into the seat opposite him. 'Believe it or not, I adored Michael. So did my mother. Is she a suspect, too?'

He pushed one of the mugs across the table. 'Hope the coffee's still hot. I wasn't going to queue twice. At the moment there is no reason to believe a crime has been committed, so no one is a suspect. Unless you know differently, of course.'

She stirred her coffee, hoping he hadn't put sugar in it. 'I just think it's odd that Michael would fall into his own pool. He knew I was coming and he'd obviously been sitting having a drink before I got there. He wouldn't be likely to go in for a swim just before I was due to arrive. Have you got the results of the post-mortem back yet?'

He shook his head. 'No, the preliminary tox screen showed something in his blood besides the alcohol, but it might have been something he took himself. They haven't identified it yet. That's something else I wanted to ask you about. I was told you still work at the hospital. You didn't tell me that.'

'Only when they need help. I occasionally fill in at the front desk if they're short-staffed. I used to work full-time but I don't like leaving my mother alone for too long.'

'What's wrong with her? She seemed fine to me.'

'Agoraphobia or something similar, the doctor isn't really sure. If she goes too far from the house she panics and can't get her breath.'

He watched her as she took a sip of her coffee. 'Did anyone see you arrive at Lansdale's house when you found him in the pool?'

'The house is up that long drive, so I have no idea whether anyone saw me. The place is in the middle of nowhere and the lanes were hardly seething with traffic.'

'In other words, no.'

The enormity of the situation suddenly hit her. 'You think Michael was murdered, don't you? I can't believe anyone would want to kill him. He was a really nice man. Besides, he's been working in Spain for ages. Years. That's how he met Debbie.'

'She was working in a bar out there. I know.' He pulled a single sheet of paper out of the stack. 'There is no evidence to suggest Michael Lansdale was murdered, but he was conducting business in Marbella, and a lot of drugs move in and out of the port. He could have upset someone'

'Are you suggesting Michael was involved in drug smuggling?'

'I told you, I'm not suggesting anything. I'm just talking to people.'

'You haven't told me how you think he was killed. There weren't any injuries on him — I would have noticed.'

'I didn't say he was killed; I'm just keeping my options open. And there *were* marks on the body — small abrasions where he might have been dragged into the water. I've already sent a team to do a sweep of the pool area, but that's as far as I can go without any evidence.' He stacked the papers and put them in a grey folder. 'We need to take your fingerprints.' He smiled, and she noticed a small dimple beside his mouth. 'Just for elimination purposes. And it would help if you could remember exactly what you touched at the house. I'll make sure your finger-prints are destroyed as soon as I take you off my list of possible suspects.'

'That's nice of you. How about the new wife? I imagine she has the most to gain from Michael's death. She should be top of your list.'

'She was in London at the time, visiting a Harley Street specialist. We have that confirmed. There's no way she could have got back in time to kill her husband, so she has the perfect alibi.' His eyes glinted. 'You, on the other hand, were right there at the scene.'

She closed her eyes for a moment. She was feeling decidedly light-headed. When she opened her eyes again she was surprised to see concern on his face.

'Are you all right? Do you need a glass of water or anything?' He leant across the table, staring at her worriedly. 'You've gone quite pale.'

She shook her head. 'No, I'm fine. It's all catching up with me, I think, and I didn't have much breakfast. I'll be OK in a minute.' Or she would be if he stopped looking at her like that. At the moment she was drowning in a sea of silver.

He eventually lowered his eyes to look at his watch. 'I can leave the forensics team to get on by themselves for another half hour. You need to eat and so do I, so I'll buy you a sandwich. Any preference?'

She shook her head. 'Chicken, tuna, cheese. I'm not fussy.'

The dimple was back. 'That's nice to hear.'

She watched him ignore the queue and speak to the manager, who went to a cabinet and came back with two packs of sandwiches. Raven paid and walked back to the table.

'You look like a brown-bread person.' He tossed her one of the packets. 'Remember to eat next time. You could have been taken ill while you were driving.'

'Debbie gave me a glass of wine, but I only drank half of it. I should have asked for a biscuit as well.' She started to unwrap her sandwich. 'I did notice something, though. There were two glasses missing from the glass-cabinet.'

'There was a wineglass on the table by the pool. We took it away for analysis, but there was nothing more sinister than a rather good Chardonnay. Why do you think there were two glasses missing?'

'Because glasses usually come in a set of six, and if only one was used there should have been five left in the cabinet.'

'Perhaps one got broken.'

She took a bite of her sandwich — tuna mayo in a soft, almost sticky malt bread. Sheer heaven. 'Maybe,' she said. 'Or maybe there *was* someone else there, like my mother said.'

4

Cass spent the weekend working on the necklace. It took her a while to fashion the centrepiece. The flower had to be solid enough to cradle a fairly large-faceted ruby. She created the flower and leaves from 14-carat-gold wire, using a single strand for the delicate veins of each leaf. Seed pearls scattered on the finished leaves would look like drops of dew.

She wanted to get the flower finished so she could take it to Debbie Lansdale. Once the leaves were edged with gold wire, and the best of the rubies polished and set in the centre of the flower, she would have a really special piece to show Michael's wife. Something the woman might actually like.

Dora liked to cook Sunday lunch and Liz had been invited. She brought a bottle of Shiraz to go with the pot-roasted beef and they started on the wine while the Yorkshire puddings rose in the oven. The doors from the living room to the patio were open wide, the room cool in spite of the heat outside, the scent of honeysuckle and pot roast mixing happily together.

Liz waited until Dora went into the kitchen to check on the food and then asked, 'Have you seen him again?'

'If you mean the policeman, yes, I have. He bought me a sandwich before asking for my fingerprints.' Cass sipped her wine. 'I'm his prime suspect at the moment because I found the body.'

'Did you go into the house?'

'I used the phone. I don't remember if I touched anything else. In fact, I don't remember much about that day. Michael's new wife was practically hysterical at the time, but when I called round to talk her about the necklace she seemed to have recovered pretty well.'

Liz moved to the edge of her seat. 'Too well?'

Cass moved her glass out of the way as her mother came back into the room and called them into the kitchen to eat. 'Debbie Lansdale is not a suspect. I've been told she has a cast-iron alibi.'

Liz snorted. 'Don't you ever watch TV? The one with the perfect alibi is always the one who did it.' She tasted her beef and moaned with pleasure. 'Dora, you are just brilliant. This is sublime.'

Dora smiled. 'Thank you, Liz.' She turned to her daughter. 'Michael was a good judge of character. I don't believe he would have made a mistake about his new wife, but I need to see her to be sure.'

Cass laughed. 'You know that is never going to happen. He probably told Debbie about your affair — Michael was nothing if not honest — so she's not likely to see you as a potential friend. I'm sure there's nothing wrong with Debbie. She's either the sort of person who copes extremely well, or she'll have a delayed reaction and suddenly go to pieces. Either way, you're not likely to get to meet her.'

'We'll see.' Dora stacked the empty plates and went to get the pudding. 'She might be just as curious about me. What's she look like? Michael never sent any photos, did he?'

'No.' Cass shook her head. 'But Michael never was one for photography; and besides, he wanted to surprise us. She's about how Michael described her, I suppose. A blue-eyed blond who looks good for her age.'

'How old is she?' Liz asked. 'You said she was a lot younger than him.'

'Thirty-two years old in a couple of weeks, and Michael was in his late sixties. That's why his son thought he was just being a silly old man, taken in by a young blond barmaid, but Debbie doesn't come across like that. Somehow I can't see her behind a Spanish bar. She looks as if she's used to something better.'

'Stereotyping,' Liz said. 'It doesn't always work.'

'She's not a barmaid now,' Dora pointed out. 'She a widow worth several million pounds.'

After dinner they sat outside on the patio in the late afternoon sunshine and Cassandra fetched her necklace centre-piece from the workshop to show her friend.

'I've still got a lot more to do. I'm going to make leaves from fourteen-carat yellow gold wire, some flower buds with a tiny cut-diamond centre, and then hang the lot on a gold chain.' She smiled. 'The lady wanted diamonds as well, so she shall have diamonds, but not very big ones.'

Dora came back from the kitchen with a pot of coffee and a jug of cream. 'Michael said Debbie was happy with the basics in life and wasn't interested in his money. Did she ask you for diamonds?'

'Not really. She just asked if I could use diamonds instead of pearls. I don't know — I'm probably over-reacting but everything seems a bit off, like looking

through the fish-eye lens of a camera.'
Cass shook her head. 'I still can't
believe Michael is dead. It doesn't make
any sense.'

'You don't know what Michael was
involved with in Spain,' Liz said. 'He
was a very rich man, and rich men
make enemies.'

'It wasn't drugs. He wouldn't get
involved in drugs. He hated the whole
idea.'

'Whatever this is,' Dora said, 'I have a
feeling it's something evil. Really evil.'

Cass was about to accuse her mother
of being ridiculous, but the words
wouldn't come. 'If Michael was killed,
his murder was planned in advance,
wasn't it? You don't just turn up at
someone's house, kill them, and then
toss them in their own pool. And he's
only been home two days. If his murder
was planned in Spain, we may never
find out what happened. Whoever did it
must have hoped it would look like an
accident.'

Liz poured cream into her coffee.

'Unless they just wanted to gain some time to catch a plane back to wherever they came from. The murderer might still have been around when you arrived, Cass. You wouldn't have noticed anything else once you saw Michael in the water.'

Cassandra felt a shiver up her spine. She had known something was wrong as soon as she got to the house. Had the murderer been watching her all the time? She thought for a moment and then shook her head. 'No, there was no one else at the house when I arrived. I would have known. The side gate was open with the alarm turned off, which was a bit odd, but Michael might have left it open for me.'

She was still feeling an overwhelming sense of guilt, coupled with all the 'ifs' that were running through her head. *If* she had arrived earlier, *if* she had tried resuscitation, *if* she had gone straight to the pool instead of standing around waiting for Michael to open the door . . . and the biggest 'if' of all — if only she could turn the clock back and start that day all over again.

There were so many unanswered questions. Perhaps she could get some answers from Noel Raven when she went to the police station to have her fingerprints taken. She didn't know how long fingerprints remained viable, but there must have been several workmen in the house at one time or another. Not counting the people who delivered the new furniture, the landscape gardeners, the people who put in the pool — the list was endless. No wonder Raven was concentrating on the pool area. It would take forever for the police to sort out the fingerprints of everyone who had been outside, let alone those who had been in the house.

As dusk settled, Dora turned on the outside lights. Cass knew there was a road at the end of the drive, and they had neighbours, but the little patio was an oasis of peace and quiet, sheltered cosily by the tall dark trees on either side. Her mother had once told her she muted the sounds beyond the fence with a spell; and if you believed that, Cass thought with a smile as she sipped her wine, you'd believe anything. But believing she was a witch kept her mother happy, and Cass had learned to go along with it.

They stayed in the garden until it began to get too cool for comfort and then went back inside the house. Dora poured more wine for herself and Cass, but Liz declined.

'I'm on duty at six a.m. tomorrow so I'd better get going. I don't want to be over the limit if that detective of yours is on the prowl.'

'He's not mine. For all I know he has a wife and three kids somewhere.'

Dora shook her head. 'He's single, but mind your step with him, Cassie. He's dangerous.'

Liz paused on her way out the door. 'Dangerous? In what way is he dangerous, Dora?'

Cass sighed. 'Don't take any notice of her, Liz. He bought me a coffee at

Costa. How dangerous is that?'

Dora shrugged. 'He knows exactly what he wants and he usually gets it.' She looked at her daughter. 'I knew this was going to happen one day, but it's too soon.'

'What *are* you talking about?' Cass said impatiently. 'You don't know anything about Noel Raven.'

'I know enough. I saw it in his eyes. He may not know it yet, but he wants you, Cassandra.'

Liz left with a laugh, but as Cass shut the door behind her friend, she wasn't laughing. Her mother never called her by her first name.

'What do you mean, he wants me?'

Dora walked into the kitchen with Cass right on her tail and started loading mugs and glasses into the dishwasher. 'I knew it would happen. I knew you'd meet someone, but I'm not sure about him. He's more powerful than he thinks.'

Cass knew her mother was talking rubbish but she still felt a little shiver run down her spine. Deep inside she knew Noel Raven was dangerous — her mother had just confirmed her suspicions.

She dressed carefully for her visit to the police station which, after all, was Noel Raven's home turf, tying her hair back in a ponytail and wearing little makeup. There was no point in drawing attention to herself; she seemed to have all she needed right now.

He met her at the door and escorted her to a room that looked like an ordinary office. There were only two people inside, a man and a girl. The man was short and bald, sweat beading his face. The girl gave Cass a sympathetic look and then went back to her computer. Once Cass was seated at a desk Raven put a sheet of card in front of her.

'This is just a standard form. I'll fill it in for you if you like, apart from your signature. I'm afraid we don't have any of the new technology here; we still do things the old way. Martin will ink your fingers and roll each one over a box on the form. It's all perfectly straight-forward.'

Cass looked at the form. One of the first questions asked for her alias. OK. And did she really want to tell this man her age and weight? No, she did not.

'I thought you just wanted my finger-prints, not a complete body identification. You must realise all women lie about their age and weight.'

'We have ways of checking.' Martin pushed over an old set of bathroom scales. 'You can leave your clothes on if you like,' he added with a leer.

'For God's sake, Martin.' Raven sounded really annoyed. 'I'll take a guess at her weight if that's what's bothering you.'

'No!' Cass held up her hand. 'No one is guessing my weight. I'd be mortified if you added pounds. Give me the pen. I'll fill the damned form in myself.' Just for fun she added an inch to her height and took a couple of pounds off her weight.

She didn't like the idea of Martin touching her and neither, evidently, did Raven. Before the other man could move, he took her hand and pressed her index finger onto the inkpad. 'I've got this, Martin. You can go back to whatever you were doing when we came in.' Looking slightly put out, the man went back to his desk.

As Raven rolled her finger across the card he lightly brushed the palm of her hand and she felt a jolt, like a mild electric shock, right down to her toes. He obviously felt it too, because he gave her a puzzled look.

'Static,' he said. 'It must be the ink.'

Yeah, that makes sense, she thought. Since when did ink transmit static electricity? He rather gingerly pressed her middle finger on the pad and when nothing happened, they both breathed a sigh of relief. There were no more electric shocks with the rest of her fingers, but getting rid of the nasty black stuff required the use of several evil-smelling wipes. When she pulled a face, Raven pointed to a sink in the corner where there was a bottle of liquid soap and a tissue dispenser.

The girl looked up from her computer. 'I provided the soap. Hawaiian nights. It's not half bad.'

Noel Raven escorted her to the door. 'I think I owe you another coffee. Shall we walk across the road to Starbucks? My treat.'

She looked up at him, wide-eyed. 'Is this a date?'

The dimple was back. 'A second date. I remember buying you coffee once before, when you had an attack of the vapours.'

She fluttered a hand in front of her face. 'It's this corset. My maid laces it up too tightly.'

He took her arm to steer her through the traffic. 'Feel free to loosen it any time. I'm not one to stand on ceremony.'

His phone buzzed while she was stirring the chocolate into her cappuccino. He listened for a few minutes, his eyes on hers. 'Right. No, I have no idea either.' He closed the phone and put it back in his pocket, looking puzzled. 'A narcotic, a sedative of some sort. A strong one by the sound of it. That doesn't make much sense, does it?'

'Sorry?' She hazarded a guess. 'Is that what they found in Michael's blood?'

'Yeah.' He stirred his own coffee slowly. 'The sort of stuff you take before you go to bed if you want to knock yourself out for the night. I'll have to find out if Lansdale had it on prescription.'

'But he was meeting me. He wouldn't put himself to sleep just before I arrived.'

'That is very true.' He sat looking at her for a long moment. 'My boss wants me to tie this up, call it accidental death and have done with it. He doesn't like the idea of a murderer on the loose. Too much paperwork involved. If we don't have any hard evidence, he wants to release the body to the family for burial or cremation.'

'But you think Michael was murdered?'

'No.' Raven shook his head. 'I'm not paid to think. I'm paid to find things out, that's why I'm called a detective. I'm just saying I can't be one hundred percent sure Lansdale's death was accidental.'

'So? What are you going to do now?'

'Find a reason to hang on to the body until I know how the man died.'

He was staring into her eyes again and she felt slightly dizzy. 'Like what?' she asked weakly.

'Evidence. Kennedy over at the lab is trying to isolate the narcotic and I've got Kevin Porter chasing Lansdale's doctor to find out if he was taking any prescribed medication. The trouble is, Lansdale might have bought something in Spain while he was over there. Maybe even got the wrong stuff by mistake, like getting a sedative or tranquilizer instead of a pain killer. How well did he speak Spanish?'

'He didn't. Well, only a few sentences. Nearly everyone speaks English. We're the lazy ones, not bothering to learn another language because we don't have to. Will they still do a post-mortem examination?'

'If it's an unexplained death, yes, but his wife is against it. I'm going to have another word with her. See if I can persuade her a PM is necessary to find out how her husband died. She must want to know, surely.'

'Maybe not. Some people just put their head in the sand. I've got to see Debbie again, as well. I promised to take the necklace to her so she can approve the stones before I finish it.'

'It's finished? I'd like to see it.'

'Really?' She was touched. 'I've got a bit more work to do on it and I went over budget, but it's my gift to Michael. He wanted something nice for his wife. Oh!' She put a hand over her mouth. 'I think I know why Debbie went to Harley Street that day. Michael mentioned in one of his emails that she wanted her boobs done and he'd spoken to a doctor he knows in London. I bet that's it.'

'Reduction or enlargement?'

'I don't know. Believe it or not, when I met Debbie I didn't stare at her boobs.'

He grinned. 'Believe it or not, neither did I.'

'You can't ask her about a breast enhancement. It's rude, and she won't tell you anyway.'

'But she'll tell you if you ask her nicely.'

'No! I'm not going to ask her, either. Women talk about most things, but that's not one of them. I wouldn't tell anyone if I had mine done.'

'Yours don't need any enhancing. They're just fine the way they are.'

She saw where he was looking and resisted the impulse to cross her arms. She couldn't stop herself blushing, though; something she thought she'd grown out of years ago. She wanted to ask him how he knew she hadn't had them done already, but she wasn't sure if she wanted to hear his answer.

He gave her a slight smile as if he could read her thoughts. 'You said

Lansdale already told you his wife was going for a consultation, so ask her how she got on. I know she went to Harley Street, and I've got the name of the consultant, but I don't know what the consultation was about. Consultants don't talk about their patients. I need to pinpoint the exact time she was there, what trains she caught, when she arrived in London and when she left. I can do all that, but if you can get any more information about what she had done, it might help.' He ran a hand through his hair. 'Dammit Cass, I need something concrete to keep this case open. If it goes down as accidental death the case is closed.'

It was the first time he had used the shortened version of her name and she felt something melt inside her. 'I'll try,' she said. 'I'll go and see Debbie tomorrow.'

'Don't ask too many questions. I don't want her to think you're interrogating her; she'll just clam up.'

Cass looked at him curiously. 'You

78

don't like her, do you?'

He shrugged. 'There are a lot of people I don't like, but that doesn't make them guilty. I discovered that a long time ago.'

She got to her feet. 'If I'm going to go rushing off to do your detective work, I'd better go home and pick up my jewellery.'

He pushed back his chair. 'Like I said, don't give her the third degree. She might get suspicious.'

Cass let him take her arm again when they crossed the road. 'She won't be suspicious. She'll just think I'm the nosiest woman she's ever met.'

5

She didn't ring first this time. She secretly hoped Debbie would be out. The grass was greener, she noted, so Debbie must have sorted out the sprinkler. Music came from somewhere round the back of the house and, after ringing the bell several times, Cass made her way to the side gate. Unbelievably, it was unlocked again and half-open. Feeling an uncomfortable sense of having done all this before, she pushed the gate open the rest of the way and walked into the garden.

The music was louder in the back, coming from speakers concealed among the rose bushes. Cass called again, but the music drowned her voice. Wishing with all her heart she didn't have to do this, she slowly made her way down the steps to the pool. What if there really was a killer walking the streets of Mickford? And what if he had come back?

Debbie was lying flat on her back on a lounger, the top half of her bikini on the table beside her. Her eyes were closed, but they popped open when Cass gave a little gasp of embarrassment.

'Dammit, you scared me!' The woman sat up and grabbed her bikini top, slipping her arms through the straps and fastening it behind her back in one practised move. 'I must have dozed off.' She reached for a remote on the table and turned down the music. 'Sorry, I wasn't expecting anyone.'

'My fault.' Cass felt mortified. She hadn't intended to creep up on Debbie while she was half-naked, or scare her to death. 'I brought the necklace round for you to look at before I finish it. I did try ringing the doorbell but you didn't answer. The gate was open and I could hear music, so I came looking for you. I'm so sorry.'

Debbie laughed. 'Stop apologising. We're both women, for goodness sake, and it's lovely to see you.' She slipped her bare feet off the lounger and stood up. 'You can tell I'm not used to visitors.'

'You should lock the back gate,' Cass said. 'Anyone could just walk in, and after what happened to Michael . . . ' Her voice tailed off. It might be a good idea, she told herself, to think before she spoke.

'I know. I should be more careful, but this place is so out of the way.' Debbie started walking towards the house with Cass following. 'I still can't believe it happened. I keep expecting Michael to walk in from the pool. It was really hot that day and he said he might have a swim. I keep remembering the last thing I said to him the day he died was goodbye.' She started up the steps. 'It looks as though I should be able to arrange the funeral soon. Someone phoned and told me they're going to release Michael's body in a few days.'

'Aren't they going to do a post-mortem? I thought that happened when a death was unexplained.'

Debbie stopped and turned to look at Cass. 'I don't want them to cut Michael. You can't imagine how that would make me feel. It was an accident, Cassandra, so whatever happens I don't believe there will be an inquest.' She started walking again. 'I phoned the crematorium this morning to ask about available dates.'

'Michael didn't want to be cremated,' Cass blurted before she could stop herself. 'He hated the idea of being burned. He wanted to be buried with his family in the old churchyard.'

'He changed his mind while he was in Spain. I'm really sorry, but he did make his wishes quite clear to me.' Debbie pushed open the sliding doors into the house. 'Would you like tea or coffee? Or I have wine, red and white. We can have a drink while I look at my lovely necklace.'

Subject obviously closed, Cass thought

with a little jolt of sadness. She was sure Michael hadn't wanted to be cremated. They had spoken about it a few years ago and he had been quite adamant. But there was always the possibility he *had* changed his mind, and it was none of her business anymore.

She chose coffee, and got espresso made in a formidable-looking machine that spat and hissed alarmingly. Debbie used tall glass beakers and frothed the milk like a professional.

'I love gadgets,' she told Cass, as they carried their coffees into the lounge. 'And I got to play with one like this when I was behind the bar.'

Debbie pushed the sliding doors all the way back and it was like sitting outside, but on an extremely comfortable sofa instead of a hard patio chair. Cass thought it must be amazing living in a house like this — but all by yourself? Maybe not so good. She remembered what she had come here for and opened her bag. The pendant was in a velvet-lined case and she had to admit, even to herself, that it looked magnificent.

The polished ruby gleamed in the centre of the flower, gold petals curving round the oval stone protectively. Seed pearls were scattered over the flower like drops of dew, and here and there a diamond glinted. Cass hadn't made the chain yet.

Debbie removed the flower from the case and smiled. 'You put in my diamonds.'

'I did. Three, actually. They may be small, but their clarity and cut is really nice. The finished necklace will look amazing on you. I still have to make the chain, but then it's finished.'

Debbie walked across the room to look in the mirror over the fireplace, holding the pendant against her skin. 'It's very pretty. Don't make the chain too long. I want the flower to show when I wear it.'

'It was from Michael. He wanted you to have something beautiful, and now you have something to remember him by as well.' She noticed the ruby had lost some of its lustre against Debbie's pale skin and decided it must be the dimness of the room. The stone needed light to look its best. 'Michael said something about another gift,' she said. 'A date with a Harley Street surgeon. Did the consultation go well?'

For a moment Debbie looked puzzled, then her face cleared. 'My augmentation. The consultation was the day Michael died. I shall never forgive myself for not being here when he fell in the pool. I didn't need to go to London. It was just a silly fantasy. Pure vanity. I've told the surgeon to put everything on hold. I may think about it again in a few months, but not now.'

'I was considering having the same thing done myself,' Cass said, trying to sound convincing, 'and I was hoping you could recommend someone, but I don't know if I could afford your guy. I can't very well split the cost and have one done at a time, can I?'

Debbie laughed. 'Hardly. But you

don't look as if you need anything done and, when I think about it, neither do I. I'm a bit too old now to start changing what nature gave me.'

'Was your op going to be with a top consultant? I just want to get an idea of how much it would cost.' Cass hoped she wasn't pushing too hard.

'Yes, I did see one of the top men, so his fee was pretty high. I told Michael there are lots of good surgeons out there, but he insisted I have the very best. You should shop around. Just make sure whoever you choose is registered. Would you like another coffee before you go?'

Cass had a feeling she was being politely dismissed and hoped she hadn't overstayed her welcome. If Raven wanted any more information he would have to get it himself. She declined the second coffee. Even a one-shot from that machine was pretty lethal.

Debbie walked Cass back to her car. 'Michael's children are arriving in a few days. I'm dreading it at the moment, but once they get here I can arrange a date for the funeral. You'll want to come, of course?'

'Of course,' Cass said. No one could keep her away from Michael's funeral. It was a pity her mother couldn't go. That would have been fun. 'My mother will be sorry she can't come, but she doesn't leave the house.'

'Your mother?'

Deborah Lansdale sounded so surprised, Cass almost laughed. So Michael hadn't told his new wife about his affair with Dora. 'My mother was quite close to Michael. I'm sure she'll miss not being there.'

'Quite close' was the understatement of the year, Cass thought as she climbed into her car. Her mobile rang when she was halfway home and there was no way she was pulling into someone's drive this time, so she ignored it. She ignored it the second time it rang, as well. She had a pretty good idea who it might be.

Her mother met her in the hallway. 'What did she think of the necklace?'

Cass kicked off her shoes and walked into the kitchen. 'She seemed quite impressed. I get to keep the cheque, anyway.' She picked up the kettle and filled it at the sink. 'I'll make tea.' She needed something to wash away the taste of the espresso coffee. 'Did Michael ever mention to you whether he wanted to be cremated or buried?'

'Buried,' Dora said, taking mugs from a cupboard. 'He felt quite strongly about it. Why?'

'Because she's having him cremated. She says he changed his mind, but I don't think they ever talked about it. They'd only known one another a short while, so you wouldn't, would you? But she's quite adamant it's going to be a cremation, and she's going to have the funeral as soon as she can. Do you think Michael might have put his wishes in his will? A lot of people do.'

Dora poured boiling water on tea bags. 'Cremation not only gets rid of the body, it also gets rid of any evidence.'

'There's no reason to think it wasn't an accident. They already tested Michael's blood and the only thing they found were traces of a sedative, which doesn't prove anything. It could have been something he took the night before.'

'So your policeman is just giving up on him?'

'He's not my policeman. And no, he's not giving up. He got me to quiz Debbie about her boob job. He wants to know the surgeon's name.'

'So she's still a suspect.' Dora handed her daughter a mug of tea. 'Raven will get to the truth in the end.'

This time, when her phone rang, Cass answered it. 'No, I didn't get the surgeon's name, but he's the best in the country, evidently, so he shouldn't be too difficult to find. Debbie's put the operation on hold for the time being. Says it was pure vanity.' Cass sipped her tea while she listened to him. 'What do you mean, do they need to be bigger? How would I know? Actually, she was topless when I arrived, and the answer to your question is no, I don't think so, but that doesn't mean anything. Look at Dolly Parton.'

Dora humphed and Cass put the phone down, looking at her mother curiously. 'What?'

'Her husband dead barely a week and she's topless by the pool. Not much mourning going on there — or was she wearing a black swimsuit?'

'Not everybody wallows around in misery for weeks on end. He was a very good friend to both of us, but we're not walking around dressed in black or crying ourselves to sleep every night, are we? It's happened. Michael's dead and nothing can change that. Maybe Debbie just wants to get on with her life.'

Dora shrugged. 'It would be polite to grieve for a few days, though.'

Cass left her mother in the kitchen and went back to her workroom. She had just received an order by email and needed to start making some rough sketches. This was an anniversary present from a man who had been married to the same woman for fifty years. Quite an achievement in this day and age, Cass thought. Roger Galloway wanted a gift for his wife that would be an expression of his love, and Cass was finding it hard to get her head around the concept. How could two people live together all that time and still be in love?

She found the stones she was looking for and tipped them onto her workbench. Rose quartz seemed particularly appropriate. The ones on her bench had all been sympathetically cut and polished to make the best of their beauty. In the end she chose a dozen perfect ovals. Drilled, and separated with gold links, they would make the basis of the necklace she was planning. One beautiful uncut stone, rose-pink and glinting with natural facets, would form the centrepiece. She hefted the polished oval stones in her hand and cut the number down to ten. She didn't want the necklace to be too heavy.

She was halfway through putting her ideas down on paper when someone knocked on the outside door. She looked up, startled. Her friends usually went to the main house first to say hello to her mother. Thinking it was probably someone trying to sell her something she didn't want, and annoyed at the interruption, she opened the door with a scowl.

'Wow,' Noel said. 'I don't usually have that effect on pretty women. Can I come in?'

She was about to say no, but he had already moved past her and was giving her workspace the once-over like the policeman he was. She closed her eyes briefly with resignation and shut the door. 'Do come in.'

He grinned at her. 'I'm already in, thank you. Nice. I expected a workshop but this is softer, more friendly.'

Now she couldn't be cross with him. 'Thank you. This is where I spend most of my time, so I like it pretty.'

He sat on her sofa and stretched out

his legs, completely at home. 'I need to talk to you about your visit to Debbie Lansdale. Do you have anything to drink?'

She found it difficult getting used to his sudden changes of subject. 'I have coffee, or beer if you prefer. Are you here on official business, or is this just a social call?'

'Do I detect a note of sarcasm? If you must make a distinction, I'm not being paid to be here, so my visit is purely social. But I still have to drive home, so a coffee would be most welcome.'

She took a packet of ground coffee from a cupboard and filled the kettle at her little sink. 'I told you everything over the phone. You didn't need to come all the way over here.' She felt his eyes on her as she spooned coffee into a cafétiere.

'Like I said, purely social. Do you mind if I look at your drawings?' The question was pointless because he had already picked up one of her sketches. 'Who's this for?'

94

'A seventy-year-old lady who's been married for fifty years.' She handed him a pale pink stone. 'Rose quartz, the stone of love.'

He rolled the stone on the palm of his hand. 'Fifty years and still in love? Aren't you being rather optimistic?' He put the polished stone back on the bench and picked up the larger, uncut one. 'I like this one. Would it have looked like this when it was first found in a mine or whatever? I suppose it's really a fossil.'

She was inordinately pleased he liked the uncut stone best. 'Once the dust was washed off, yes, it would have gleamed just like that. A pretty thing in a big, ugly lump of rock.'

He lifted his eyes from the stone to look at her. 'That happens sometimes. A pretty thing where you least expect it.' He put the stone he was holding back with the others and picked up the mug of coffee she had put beside him. 'Go over your conversation with Debbie Lansdale one step at a time. How on earth did you bring up the subject of breast implants?'

'I told her I was thinking of having the same thing done myself, and asked her if she could recommend anyone. She wouldn't actually give me the name of her surgeon, but I'm sure you can find out who he is.' Cass started packing away her stones. 'She's going to have Michael cremated, and I know he wanted to be buried, but I suppose she can do what she likes.'

'Unless he mentioned it in his will, or specifically stated his wishes to either of his children, yes, she probably can.'

'Are they going to do a post-mortem?'

'They weren't, but I managed to convince the coroner otherwise. It's scheduled for tomorrow. If they don't find anything suspicious we have to release the body back to his wife.' He ran his eyes over her thoughtfully. 'You weren't, were you?'

'Sorry?' He was changing course mid-stream again.

'Thinking of having a boob job. You don't need anything changed.' When she was about to speak, he held up his hand. 'Just making a point.'

'Michael's two children arrive in a couple of days. I haven't seen them for ages, but Debbie seems to think she's going to have trouble with Michael's son. He thought his father was being ridiculous, wanting to get married again, and then choosing someone nearly half his age.'

'Can't blame him. Colin Lansdale is almost thirty-eight, so his stepmother is younger than he is. It must feel a bit weird; and besides, he probably thought his dad was being conned. The old boy was worth a few millions.'

'You've been doing your homework.'

'No, just doing my job. I wonder just how deep the resentment went. Colin Lansdale phoned his father a few days ago and the conversation only lasted a couple of minutes, which makes me think someone got annoyed and hung up.'

'That's stretching it a bit. Perhaps someone came to the door — or the toast popped up. Anything could have happened.' She finished her coffee and took his empty mug when he held it out to her, standing them on the worktop. 'I thought you could hack into phones and find out what people are talking about.'

'Believe it or not, that's illegal. I'd need a warrant to listen to someone else's phone call. On the other hand, I suppose I could just ask him. Are the two offspring staying at the Lansdale house or a hotel?'

'I have no idea. Debbie doesn't seem the type to confide in anyone. I used to be close to Michael when I was a child, but he's been abroad on and off for years, the last five in Spain.'

She wasn't going to tell him Michael had left the country when Dora turned down his marriage proposal. Cass had kept in touch via email and had enjoyed hearing about his travels, but for the last year, since he met Debbie, the emails had tailed off. Cass had been as shocked as everyone else when Michael said he was getting married again.

'He was widowed, wasn't he? From what I hear, he was a rich man. It's a wonder he managed to keep out of the clutches of all those predatory females out there.'

'I think he came close a couple of times.' Cass knew Michael had been in love with her mother, and Dora would be hard to replicate. 'He was quite savvy where women were concerned. He wasn't the sort of person to be taken in very easily, and he seemed to think Debbie was the genuine article.'

'And you don't?'

Cass avoided his eyes. 'I didn't say that. She seems a very nice woman. I'm sure she would have made Michael a good wife if she'd had the chance.'

He shook his head. 'Not convincing, I'm afraid. You're avoiding the question. It's a pain, isn't it, when you really don't like someone but can't put your finger on why.' Without a pause, he said, 'I'm going over there tomorrow.'

'To see his children?' She was getting used to guessing where his thoughts had gone. 'They may not be staying with her.'

'Then I'll find out where they are staying. You're going to the funeral, I take it? Even if you do think she's going against his wishes.'

'Yes, of course.' Cass chewed her bottom lip. 'Do you know when Michael's will is likely to be read?'

'It would have to be in front of the beneficiaries, I would think, so any time Lansdale's family are all in one place. Any other beneficiaries would be notified and asked to attend as well.' Raven picked up his jacket and walked towards the door. 'Do you know if he changed his will recently? After he got married?'

'People do when they get married. He would have wanted to make Debbie his main beneficiary. Leave her the house and most of everything else.'

The detective turned with his hand

on the door handle. 'But what if he didn't? What if he was waiting until he got back to England, and hadn't had time?'

'Then she'd have no reason to kill him, would she?'

'Maybe not, but his children would have a pretty good motive.'

6

Noel Raven sat in his office and read the coroner's report for the third time.

When he first took over, the desk had been directly opposite the glass door into the outer office. His predecessor obviously liked to see what was going on. But Noel found that worked both ways and everyone in the outside room could also see him. He didn't like the idea of being the centre of attention, so the first thing he did was move his desk slightly to the right. Now he only had to tilt his head to see everything he wanted, but no one could see him unless they came right up to the door and looked in.

Was there enough evidence for an inquest? Probably not. Traces of a sedative in the victim's blood and grazes on his legs weren't enough. Michael Lansdale could have taken the sedative the night before, and the grazes could have happened when he fell into the pool or, alternatively, tried to stop himself falling in. He might even have been walking up the steps to get out of the water and felt faint. The forensics team had done a thorough job on the area round the pool, but the only traceable fingerprints on the glass table top belonged to Michael Lansdale. All except one, and that could have belonged to anyone. There was no trace of it in any records.

Noel leaned back in his chair. There should have been more than one fingerprint on a glass table. Surely Michael Lansdale would have touched the table when he put his glass down. The table had been cleaned, that was pretty obvious, but had it been cleaned before or after Lansdale died, that was the question. He knew the couple had advertised for someone to help in the house but, as far as he knew, no one had applied for the job.

When he called at the house Mrs

Lansdale had been polite and helpful, giving a clear and precise account of her arrival back at the house on the day of her husband's accident. He asked her where she had been, and she told him she had been to Harley Street in London to have a consultation with a surgeon. She didn't volunteer any details, but she didn't appear to be lying or holding anything back. Noel had the man's name and the time of the appointment in front of him, now confirmed. As cast-iron alibis go, it was a beauty.

He pushed the report away. There had been no need for Cassandra Moon to question Debbie Lansdale. He had just wanted to see if she would do it, and there was always the chance Debbie would tell things to another woman she wouldn't tell a man. Now he had to wait and see what would happen when Lansdale's offspring met their stepmother for the first time. That should definitely be interesting.

He looked up when Kevin came in to

his office. The young detective looked pleased with himself.

'I know you said it wasn't worth doing a house-to-house, but the Lansdales only have two neighbours, so I gave them a knock. Only one of them was in when I called and I made the excuse we were doing a routine check on security in the area. She told me the man in the new house at the end of the drive had died a couple of days ago, so not to call there.'

He paused for breath and Noel felt his impatience building. He didn't need a detailed police report; he just needed the information that was making Kevin Green look like the Cheshire Cat. 'So? What is this about, Kevin?'

'I asked her if she'd seen anything suspicious or any suspicious characters around in the last few days. She told me she saw the Lansdales' four-by-four leave the house on the day of the accident.' He paused for effect. 'At just before two o'clock in the afternoon.'

Noel shook his head. 'No, Mrs

Lansdale left the house earlier than that.' He found the file he was looking for. 'In her statement she says her appointment in Harley Street was at two p.m. and took an hour. Then she caught the three-thirty p.m. train home.' He looked up at Kevin. 'I know she kept her appointment because I spoke to the receptionist, so even if she was lying through her teeth about the train times she couldn't have kept her appointment and got back before Cassandra Moon arrived at three p.m. I also have a report here that says Lansdale had already been dead at least an hour before Cassandra Moon arrived.'

Kevin's grin wavered. 'This woman, a Mrs Burton, is positive it was the Lansdales' car. She says she hates those big gas-guzzlers. She only sort of mentioned seeing the car in passing and I didn't want to cross-examine her about it, but she seems pretty sure it was their car.'

Noel sat back in his chair and clasped

his hands, pressing the tips of his thumbs together. 'It couldn't have been. Besides, the Lansdale car is black, and there must be hundreds of black utilities driving around Norton. Any one of them could have had a reason to call at the Lansdale house at that particular time.'

Kevin's smile slipped a little more. 'I know. Hell of a coincidence, though, isn't it?'

'How old is this Mrs Burton?'

'Probably in her sixties, but definitely not senile.'

Noel shrugged. Much as he wanted new evidence, he didn't intend to clutch at any straw that presented itself. 'She doesn't need to be senile — just short-sighted. It's not enough for an inquest, Kevin.'

'I suppose it could have been the jeweller's car she saw.'

Noel shook his head. 'Cassandra Moon has a white Mini. No way they could be mistaken. Write it up and leave the report on my desk. All we can do is keep a note of everything that pops up. There's nothing in the pathology report to suggest anything other than a tragic accident. However — ' He waved the report in the air. ' — there are a number of little things that might add up to something much bigger. Like the grazing on Lansdale's legs, mainly on his knees and the tops of his toes; traces of a sedative, not enough to kill him but enough to put him to sleep; a missing wineglass from the set in the lounge; and now a strange car round about the time of death. It's a puzzle, Kevin, and that's what we do. Solve puzzles.'

As Kevin left the room Noel remembered there was something else. He opened the file and took out the report from the forensic team. The wineglass and the bottle had Michael Lansdale's fingerprints all over them — no one else's — but an unidentified fingerprint had been found on the table top. A fingerprint made by a woman. Someone other than Debbie Lansdale or Cassandra Moon. Maybe Dora

Moon was right, and there had been someone else at the house that day. Perhaps he should have another word with the witch and take what she said a little more seriously — or was he just trying to think of an excuse to see her auburn-haired daughter again?

Something tickled at the back of his mind. Something he'd seen and forgotten. Still clasping his hands, he rolled his thumbs round one another. The thought was there; all he had to do was get hold of it. He closed his eyes and went back to the beginning, the area around the swimming pool, the scene of Lansdale's death. But all he could remember clearly was Cassandra Moon, her wet clothes clinging to her, rising out of the water like Aphrodite. He opened his eyes and found the sheet of paper he was looking for, a list of items. Sun loungers with foam mattresses and matching cushions; two small glass-topped tables; a yellow inflatable lilo; a wine bottle and a glass, now removed for evidence; and Lansdale's towel and sunglasses, also taken away for evidence.

Maybe his problem lay inside the house. The décor was too stark and minimalist for his taste. He much preferred Dora's kitchen. He had found out her birth name was Pandora, and that intrigued him. Cassandra and Pandora. From what he could remember, Cassandra told stories that were never believed, and Pandora opened a forbidden box and let all the evil escape out into the world. Quite a pair.

Noel got to his feet and walked into the outer office. 'I'm going out for a bit.'

He drove to the Lansdale house on the off-chance someone would be home. He wanted to speak to Debbie Lansdale, mainly to see if talking to her again jogged his memory, and at some point he had to interview Michael's children. That should really be done at the police station, but he usually found people more relaxed in a home environment. Maybe not this home, though.

Debbie met him at the front door. She was dressed in tight jeans and a silky top in pale lemon. The little studs in her ears looked like real diamonds and the watch on her wrist had a Rolex logo. There wasn't much resemblance to a Spanish barmaid, but some women learn fast.

'Have you found out something? Is that why you're here?'

'No, nothing new. I wanted to ask you a few more questions. Mainly about your time in Spain.' He saw her relax, and wondered what she had been worried about. Obviously not about questions relating to Spain. 'Are Colin and Emma here?'

'No, they're not. Colin still wants his father to be buried. The solicitor read the will and there's no mention of Michael's wishes either way, so I really don't know what his problem is.' She took Noel's arm and drew him inside the house. 'They've gone to see the solicitor again. I want to get the date for the funeral sorted as soon as possible but Colin is holding things up. Quite deliberately, I think.'

'I'd like to speak to them both, but there's no hurry. I gather neither of them has seen their father for some time.'

'No, which is exactly my point. How could they possibly know what Michael's wishes were? I told them I'm happy to have their input, but now they're here they want to take over.' She reached into a box on the coffee table and took out a cigarette. 'Michael didn't like me smoking, but I need something to take my mind off all the hassle I'm getting at the moment.'

She lit the cigarette with a gold lighter she took from her bag, and Noel wondered where that had come from. Certainly not from Michael if he didn't like her smoking. He looked round the room and found it just as bare as when he'd first seen it. He had expected Debbie to have a few of her own things around by now; surely she must have a few bits and bobs she had brought with her from Spain. But there was nothing, and it was then that it struck him — there were no photographs.

His mother's house had photographs everywhere, and he had seen a few in Pandora's kitchen, but maybe he was just being old-fashioned. He knew if he was going to start a new life he would want a few photos of his old one, but perhaps people just took an iPad with them now.

He waited while Debbie poured herself a glass of wine, refusing one himself. 'Thanks, but I'm on duty. Can I ask if you've thought of anything you haven't told us? There are a few anomalies to do with your husband's death. It wasn't as straightforward as we first thought.'

Some of the colour left the woman's face, but she stubbed out her cigarette with a steady hand. 'I don't think I understand what you mean. Michael fell in the pool and drowned.'

'No, he didn't drown. He was dead before he went into the water. His heart is sound and he didn't have a stroke, so his fall was unlikely to have been caused by a medical condition. A fairly strong dose of a sedative was found in his blood, and there were some unusual marks on his legs that need investigating. I'm not talking about anything suspicious, Mrs Lansdale.' *Not yet anyway*, Noel thought. 'But we have enough evidence to look into the case further.'

Debbie finished her drink in one go, and Noel wondered if he had been a bit too blunt. For some reason he wanted to shake the woman up a bit. After her little display of histrionics by the pool, she was taking her new husband's death a bit too calmly. He wanted to see some emotion for once, but she soon had herself under control again. Putting down her glass, she took another cigarette from the box.

'There are drug dealers in Marbella,' she said. 'Particularly in Puerto Banus, and I think Michael may have been mixed up in something. Something dangerous. When we got back home one night someone had been in the house. And I'm sure I was followed a couple of times.'

'You think someone followed Michael to England and killed him?' Noel tried to keep the scepticism out of his voice, but he was finding it difficult. If the man had been mixed up in drug smuggling, he deserved all he got, but Debbie had never mentioned anything to do with drugs before. Neither had Cass or her mother. The fact that neither of them had seen Lansdale for a while could have something to do with that, he decided. It's not the sort of thing you casually mention in an email.

'It could happen, couldn't it?' Debbie sucked hard on her cigarette. 'I mean, what if he owed some of those men money?'

'Do you think he did? If you seriously think Michael owed a drug dealer money, and that was why he was found dead in his own pool, you need to tell me everything you know about it.'

'I don't know anything. Well, I mean, nothing for certain. I just thought that might be the reason he was killed.'

'I didn't say he was killed, Mrs Lansdale. I told you we were investigating further.'

'Of course you did. I'm just being silly.' She got to her feet and stubbed out her half-smoked cigarette. 'I'm sure you have other things to do, Mr Raven. I'll tell Colin and Emma you called.'

He wasn't done yet, and he didn't like being dismissed like a doorstep salesman. 'We need all the information you have on the intruder in your house in Spain, and a description of the person who followed you home. If you can find the time, it would be a good idea if you came to the police station and worked with a police artist. You might remember more that way.'

'I didn't actually see anyone.' She reached towards the cigarette box again, but then changed her mind. 'I told you it was just a feeling. And we didn't call the police about the intruder

116

because we weren't entirely sure anyone had been inside the house. Again, it was just a feeling.'

He had a feeling, too. That the damn woman was making things up as she went along. Why, he had no idea, but he intended to find out.

★ ★ ★

Cass hadn't heard from anyone besides Liz for almost a week. Her friend was working three long nights in a row, so even when she was awake she would still be half-asleep. There was no point in going out for a meal because Liz would be too tired to eat, and any sort of alcohol was out of the question. Cass was feeling edgy and bored. It had taken her weeks to design and create the ruby necklace, but now it was finished she felt lost, as if something beautiful was about to go from her life. She tried very hard not to get personally attached to the pieces she made, but sometimes it just happened, and she hated the thought of handing the ruby over to someone who might not appreciate it.

Then, two days later, she got a phone call from Debbie. 'I've finished the necklace,' she said, before the woman could have a go at her. 'Actually, I finished the chain a week ago, but I needed to clean it up.' She had intended to hang on to the necklace until Debbie's birthday, because that was what Michael would have done, but she knew Debbie was anxious to see the finished article.

'I wasn't calling about the necklace,' Debbie said. 'Michael's children are here, and I was going to ask if you'd like to come over and meet them.' She paused. 'I could do with some support, and you might be able to convince Colin I'm not the wicked stepmother.'

Her voice hitched on the last couple of words, and Cass felt guilty for not phoning sooner. 'Of course I'll come. I'd love to meet them. I haven't seen either of them for years. I'll drop by tomorrow afternoon and bring the necklace with me.'

She wanted to see Michael's children again and was quite happy to go to the house, but the woman had sounded as if she was about to burst into tears, and Cass didn't want to be on the line when that happened. She made a feeble excuse about a knock on the door and put the phone down. Then she went to find her mother.

'They call her the wicked stepmother, do they?' Dora stirred some dark green concoction she was cooking, her back to the room, but Cass had a feeling her mother was smiling. 'Does the name fit, do you think?'

'No — Oh, I don't know. I very much doubt Colin called her that to her face, although he could always be a bit antsy for no reason. Debbie wouldn't have to do anything to annoy him. He disliked her before he even met her.' When Dora muttered over her stew, Cass frowned at her. 'What did you say?'

'Just that I disliked her before I even met her, as well. Michael had no business marrying her. He promised me he wouldn't do anything stupid, and then he goes and marries some woman he hardly knows.'

Cass sighed. 'So you're jealous of Debbie, and Colin hates her. The poor woman doesn't stand a chance.'

Dora lifted some limp green dangly things from the pot and studied them carefully before dropping them back in. 'I'm not jealous of her, but it was a mistake, Cassie. He made a terrible mistake and now he's suffered the consequences.'

'You think his death had something to do with him getting married to Debbie?'

'Of course. What else could it be?' Dora wiped her hands on her apron. 'I need to meet her. You must get her to come here, to this house. I need to see her to know exactly what's going on.'

'She won't want to meet you. You're like an ex-wife.'

'That's why she *will* want to meet me. Ask her when you see her tomorrow. She'll say yes.'

Cass looked suspiciously at the pot on the stove. 'If she does come here, no spells.'

Dora stirred her green stew. 'No spells.'

Cass started setting the kitchen table for lunch, wondering why she had asked such an inane question. Her mother made herbal remedies, not spells.

After a quick lunch of salad and homemade quiche, Cass went back to her studio and took the necklace out of its velvet bag. The gold chain she had chosen complemented the pendant perfectly, but even though it was exactly as she had envisaged it, and quite beautiful, she still wasn't completely happy with it. It didn't seem quite finished. The ruby glistened in the overhead studio light, but she remembered how dull it had looked when Debbie picked it up. A ruby only shines for the person it belongs to; that means someone born at the correct time on the astrological chart, usually in July.

Debbie was born right in the middle of the month, so there shouldn't be a problem; but there was, and Cass had no idea why. She didn't usually make mistakes with her stones and it bothered her when she did. She dropped the necklace into the bag and put it back in the safe.

A couple of times she had thought of calling Noel Raven. She didn't know if Michael's body had been released for burial, or whether Debbie had won her battle and Michael was going to be cremated. She could think of all sorts of sinister reasons for Debbie to want Michael's body burned, but she knew that was partly because of her mother's insistence that he'd been murdered.

She wandered back into the kitchen to find Dora stirring yet another saucepan of greenish goo. Cass sniffed the pot and decided that, actually, the stuff didn't smell too bad; a mix of herbs and spices that was quite pleasant. Dora stopped stirring and looked up at her daughter.

'In case you're wondering, it's a

potion for a skin allergy, not a spell.'

'Thank goodness for that. It smells strong enough to turn someone into a frog.'

Dora continued her stirring. 'There's something I need to tell your policeman.'

Cass looked at her mother in surprise. 'What could you possibly want to tell Noel?'

'Someone took a taxi from the station to the corner of Barleycorn Lane the day Michael was killed. It was on Facebook. A woman called the taxi just after midday. A woman with a suitcase.'

'I'm sorry, but I don't understand why that should interest Noel. There are several houses in that area. She could have been going anywhere. If she was on her way to kill Michael she'd hardly have a suitcase with her, would she?'

'I didn't say she killed him, but she's connected to him in some way.'

Cass sighed. 'You can't possibly know that, but she might have seen something, I suppose. Someone hanging around, or going down the lane to the house. Did any of your Facebook friends inform the police?'

'I don't think so. Noel needs to find out where the woman was going. You have to call him.'

'I can't tell him how to do his job, Mother. Besides, he's working. He'll be too busy to talk to me.'

'No, he won't. Just tell him this is all part of the same thing.'

Cass gave a little sigh of exasperation. 'Was that on Facebook, too?'

Dora pulled her apron over her head and smoothed her hair. Her face was pink from the stove and little beads of sweat dotted her upper lip. 'Please ask him to come here, Cassie. I need to speak to him.'

'You phone him, then.'

'I did say please.'

Cass looked at her mother curiously. It was unlike Dora to beg for anything. She picked up the phone and rang the police station. With a bit of luck Noel would be out investigating something really important.

He picked up on the first ring. 'Hi, Cass.'

Shocked into silence, she heard him laugh.

'No, I haven't suddenly acquired psychic abilities. I have a new phone with caller ID.'

'My mother says someone got out of a taxi on the corner of Barleycorn Lane on the day Michael was killed. She says it was mentioned on Facebook and she wants to talk to you.'

'I'll be right over.'

'I don't suppose it's anything important, really,' Cass said apologetically. 'You've met Dora, so you know what she's like. She says it's all part of the same thing, whatever that means.'

'Like I said, I'll be right over.'

Cass frowned at the phone as she put it back on its stand. 'He said he'll be right over.'

Dora picked up the kettle. 'Good, I'll make a pot of tea.'

7

Noel didn't break any speed records, but he didn't drive slowly, either. He thought whatever Dora had to tell him might possibly be important and he had to follow up all leads, although had no idea why she might know anything significant. According to her daughter, Dora was bordering on doolally, but for some reason he believed most of what the strange little woman told him — which was probably rather irresponsible for a detective inspector, particularly if the woman in question was a witch.

Smiling to himself, he parked outside the house in the shadowy driveway and approached the front door. The paint on the door looked darker today, more burgundy than red; and as he reached for the bird-shaped knocker he saw the glint of a bright green eye. Startled, he withdrew his hand. One of Cass's gemstones, no doubt, but he was surprised he hadn't noticed it before. Changing his mind about knocking on the front door, he headed round the back.

'Sorry to barge in, but the door was unlocked,' he said by way of explanation. 'I believe you wanted to tell me something, Dora.'

Dora smiled smugly. 'See, Cassie? I told you he'd come. I've just made tea, Noel. Can I get you a cup?'

'It *is* proper tea,' Cass told him. 'Not her usual herbal rubbish.'

Dora poured the tea into a small bone-china cup, adding milk before she handed it to him. 'The wife of the local taxi driver said he dropped off a woman at about lunchtime. She had a suitcase with her.'

'And this was at the top of the lane leading to the Lansdales' house?'

'Yes. The taxi driver's wife is the village gossip. If anyone gets up to anything in Bob's taxi, his wife posts it on Facebook an hour later.'

Noel pulled out a chair and joined them at the table. 'I've had men door-knocking, but I never thought to check Facebook.' He took his phone out of his pocket. 'What's the name of the woman who posted the message?'

Dora shook her head. 'Glenda Fry is her real name, but people often use false names on Facebook.'

Noel grinned. 'I'm not surprised. I would imagine she could be in a lot of trouble if she used her real name.' He didn't ask how Dora knew the woman's name. He wasn't sure he would believe the answer.

He saw Cass watching him worriedly as he spoke to Kevin. The call didn't take long.

'Don't worry. I didn't say where I got the information. When Kevin calls on Mrs Fry he'll say it's part of a routine house-to-house enquiry. If the woman is as nosy as you say, Dora, she might know where the woman was going. I don't hold out much hope, but nothing makes much sense at the moment.'

Pandora looked across the table at him, her head to one side. 'Why did you come in the back door, Noel?'

He pretended not to understand. 'I thought you'd most likely be in the kitchen.'

'Last time you came here you knocked on the front door.'

He laughed, trying to make it sound light. 'You know me now; I'm a regular visitor, so I didn't think you'd mind me coming in the back door. Besides, I don't like your bird knocker.' He took a gulp of too-hot tea and winced. 'While we're on the subject, since when did it have a glass eye?'

Cass frowned. 'It hasn't got a glass eye. It's just an old iron knocker.'

Dora reached across the table and put her hand over his. Her hand was as light as a feather, warm and dry. 'You didn't touch the raven, did you, Noel.'

The way she said it, he wasn't sure if she was asking a question or making a statement. 'No, I didn't touch it.'

'Good.' She removed her hand and

smiled at him. 'No harm done, then.'

Cass frowned, and he thought she still looked good even with a furrow of lines between her brows. 'Have you been mucking about with the door knocker, Mother? That thing is an heirloom. It came with the house.'

'No, it didn't,' Dora said. 'It arrived the same time we did. But no matter. If Noel can spot the signs he will be able to avoid any problems.'

He watched Cass push her chair back and collect the empty cups. She was still frowning and still obviously irritated with her mother. 'Noel is busy, Mother. Talking in riddles isn't going to help.'

Unfazed, Dora smiled at him and topped up his cup with more tea. 'I'm sure the woman with the suitcase has something to do with Michael's murder.'

'There was a black car similar to the Lansdales' four-by-four seen driving around a little later. The woman who got out of the taxi might have seen it. That would tie up another loose end.'

He took another sip of his tea. It was cooler now. Hot, and faintly aromatic. Different, but nice. 'When are you seeing Mrs Lansdale again?' he asked Cass.

'I'm going over there tomorrow. I promised I'd take the necklace round in the afternoon. Why?'

'Perhaps you could report back to me and let me know how Colin and Emma Lansdale are getting on with their stepmother. It seems there is some sort of family feud going on about the funeral. I'd call on her again myself, but she wasn't too happy with me when I saw her last time. It would be bordering on harassment to call again so soon.'

Cass smiled at him, and he was glad to see the worry lines had gone. 'And that bothers you? I find that hard to believe. Perhaps a little harassment would make Debbie Lansdale tell the truth. She's lying about something.'

'I know. That's why I need your help.' He had a feeling Cass could spot a lie from quite a distance. Stick to the facts, he told himself. She wouldn't respond to flattery.

'OK, Mr Raven. I'll see what I can do. Don't I get a deputy's badge, or something?'

He grinned at her. 'I'll see what I can do, Miss Moon.'

Dora asked him to stay for dinner, but he reluctantly declined. He wanted to follow up on the Facebook lead. It wasn't lack of leads that was bothering him — he had more leads than he knew what to do with — but he was still missing a vital piece of the puzzle.

As he walked round the side of the house towards his car, he thought about having another look at the door-knocker, but he didn't. Pandora had called it a raven, but it could be any sort of bird. Any bird that belonged to the crow family. There were a lot of large black birds that looked like the one on the door-knocker.

By the time he got back to his office, Kevin and Brenda had found the Facebook witness. 'The woman really is a chatterbox,' Brenda said. 'She was really excited to have the police call on her and she didn't stop talking.'

'Her husband was out, needless to say,' Kevin added. 'We told her he wouldn't know we'd called on her unless she told him herself.'

'All she really knows is that her husband dropped off a woman with a suitcase at about twelve-thirty p.m. on the day Lansdale died. The woman didn't want to talk while she was in the taxi and when he asked where to drop her off, she said somewhere near Barleycorn Lane.'

'Did he see which direction she took when she got out of the taxi?'

'No, he didn't. His wife, being nosy, asked him where the woman was going, and he said he had no idea. He let her out of the cab and she stayed where she was until he'd driven off.'

Noel rubbed a hand across his face. 'It's still all hearsay, then, isn't it? Second-hand knowledge. We can't be sure the woman in the taxi had anything to do with Michael Lansdale's death, and we're not likely to find the black four-track that was being driven around the village while Debbie Lansdale was in London. Big black cars are a common sight pretty well anywhere.'

'It might be worth speaking to someone at the Harley Street clinic in person,' Kevin suggested. 'Rather than just talking to someone on the phone. I spoke to a receptionist who confirmed Mrs Lansdale had kept her appointment, but she was reluctant to tell me anything more because all their records are confidential. She said she knew for certain the appointment had been kept because it was crossed through in the book.'

'Anyone could have crossed the name through,' Brenda said.

Noel steepled his hands. 'So her alibi might not be as watertight as we first thought.'

'Tell me again?' Brenda asked. 'Why is she still our number-one suspect?'

Noel smiled without a great deal of

humour. 'Because she's the only one we've got.'

'We ought to do one of those boards on the wall, like they do on television,' Kevin suggested. 'You know, lots of pictures and clues.'

'You find me lots of pictures and clues and I promise I'll do a board like they have on TV.' He swivelled his chair and stared out of the window at the street below. 'There was something about the area around the pool. Something missing. It's been bugging me for days.'

'A cushion,' Brenda said. 'There were four loungers, but only three cushions. One was missing.'

Noel slapped his hand against his forehead. 'Now she tells me!'

Brenda shrugged. 'You didn't ask me before. I'm not a mind-reader. There was a wineglass missing, too.'

'Yes, I know. Cassandra mentioned that. So we could have a scenario where Michael Lansdale was given a sedative in his glass of wine, hence the missing glass, and was then smothered with the missing cushion.'

'All done by the missing suspect,' Brenda said dryly. 'And all pure hypothesis.'

Noel frowned at her. 'Spoilsport. Go and get me some facts, then.'

'And what are you intending to do while we're out hunting up these facts, if you don't mind my asking?'

'Not at all. I'm going undercover to visit to the boob clinic. I shall wear dark glasses and a false moustache, and you can come with me as my wife and pretend you're interested in having some implants.'

Brenda shook her head in disbelief. 'Have you looked at my boobs lately?'

Noel leered at her. 'All the time, sweetheart.' He held up his hands in surrender. 'OK, I can see you don't need enhancing. Perhaps they do reductions as well.'

Brenda raised a disbelieving eyebrow. '*Now* what are you implying?'

Kevin sniggered and Noel closed his

eyes. 'Forget I mentioned the subject. No one at the clinic is going to tell a police officer anything, not without a disclosure order, and for that I need evidence. I thought I might get more information as a concerned husband, rather than a policeman, but I can see that's not going to work.'

'Perhaps the clinic does male enhancements as well,' Barbara said dryly. 'Then you can go all by yourself.'

'Get out of my office, both of you. It's lunchtime. If anyone's getting sandwiches, I'll have a BLT with pickle.'

After they left the room, Noel stared out of the window at the people on the street below. Police work was like putting together a jigsaw puzzle. Once all the pieces were in the right order, the rest would be comparatively easy.

* * *

Cass drove slowly down the lane to Michael's house. The sun was blazing from a clear blue sky and it should have

137

been a pleasant journey, but she wished she was visiting Michael and his new wife for the first time. It would be nice to call on some of those powers her mother kept on telling her she had, and turn back time, but clicking her heels together didn't seem to work. As she parked in front of the house she saw a car she didn't recognise. Colin and Emma were inside with Debbie. Cass felt her stomach give one of those little flips that comes with a bout of nerves. She took a couple of deep breaths. What was the matter with her? She was among friends here, not walking into an enemy camp.

Before she had time to lock the car, the front door opened and Emma came running towards her with a big smile on her face. Emma was ten years younger than her brother, only a few months older than Cass, and at one time they had been like sisters. Emma's mother had coped quite well with her first child, but after she had Emma she suffered severe depression and finished up in a care home. She died a few years later and Dora had become a substitute mother for the little girl.

Emma hugged her friend. 'Cassie! It's lovely to see you. I'm always meaning to email. We promise to keep in touch, but we never do.'

'I'm as guilty as you are. Where's your brother?'

'In the house.' She lowered her voice. 'I wanted to have a word with you before we went in. Have you met Debbie? What do you think of her?'

'She seems nice.' Cass knew she was hedging, but if Emma was getting along with her stepmother she didn't want to cause a problem.

Emma shook her head. 'I don't think she *is* nice. I think she just pretends to be nice. I don't know why Daddy married her. Do you think she's after his money?'

'Debbie told me you two were getting along really well.'

'Good. I'm glad she said that. It proves I can act. Colin deliberately annoys her all the time, but I can't see the point. I know Daddy wanted us to get on, so I shall do my best. I'm pretty sure he wanted to be buried next to Mummy, and Debbie's going to have him cremated, but he won't care now, will he? So there's no point in arguing about it.'

Cass was about to agree when Debbie appeared in the doorway. 'Come on inside, you two. It's too hot to stay out in the sun. You can catch up on your gossip later.' She smiled at Cass. 'Besides, I'm dying to see my necklace now it's finished.'

Air conditioning was keeping the big room cool, even though the glass doors were pushed right back. Outside the pool was almost too blue, glinting in the afternoon sunshine, heat waves rising visibly from the sun-baked patio. Colin was sitting on one of the white leather sofas. He looked relaxed, but Cass could see tension in the stiff lines of his body. She had a feeling there was going to be trouble before the day was out, and she really didn't want to be around when it happened.

She undid her bag and took out the velvet pouch. Sitting down beside Colin, she tipped the necklace out onto the table. A ray of sunshine appeared from nowhere and caught the natural faceting of the ruby in a gleam of fire. Emma gasped.

'Oh, my! It's so beautiful. May I touch it?'

After a quick glance at Debbie, Cass nodded. She watched Emma pick up the necklace and hold it with something bordering on reverence. Even out of the sun, the stone still glowed with a light of its own. Cass was absurdly pleased with Emma's reaction. It was what she had hoped for from Debbie.

Colin smiled at his sister. 'It would look good on you, Em. Pity you can't afford it. It suits you.'

'Yes, it does.' Debbie held out her hand. 'But I want to see what it looks like on me.' Reluctantly, Emma handed the necklace to her stepmother.

'Shall I do up the clasp for you?' Cass asked. As the ruby touched Debbie's bare skin, she saw the woman start. 'Is something wrong?'

Debbie put her hand over the pendant. 'I'm not sure.'

'It's been professionally polished. There aren't any sharp edges to hurt you.' Cass lifted the stone from where it rested above the low neckline of Debbie's dress and was surprised to see a patch of skin that looked faintly pink. 'Did something hurt you? I'm sorry.'

Debbie shook her head. 'For a moment the stone felt quite warm, but it's fine now.'

'I'll take it back and check the gold wire. It's possible I left an end exposed.' She was quite sure she hadn't, but there was no harm in making absolutely sure. Something had made a mark on Debbie's neck and she didn't want to be sued for bodily injury. 'You shouldn't have it until your birthday, anyway,' she added with a smile. 'And that's over a week away.' She unclasped the gold chain and removed the necklace, slipping it back into the velvet bag.

'The ruby is my birthstone, too,' Emma said. 'If I get a part on television and become famous, I'll get you to make me something similar.' Emma acted in small local plays and did quite well, but she had been trying to get into television for years.

'The eighteenth of July,' Cass said. 'Did you think I'd forgotten?'

'No.' Emma smiled. 'You may forget to visit or email, but you always send me a card on my birthday.'

The next half hour passed in relative calm. Debbie had made a punch with fruit juice, white wine and lots of ice. Even Colin managed to join in the small talk. Nobody mentioned the funeral and Cass was glad about that, but she wished they could talk about Michael. Everyone seemed to be frightened of mentioning his name. Debbie had been a big part of the last year of his life, and Cass wanted to know what had drawn them together. Michael had always been warm and funny and interesting, and Debbie seemed none of those things. But first impressions are often wrong, and the woman had recently become a widow. She was probably still in shock.

In the end it was Emma who put an end to the idle chat. 'When are they going to let us make arrangements for Daddy's funeral?' she asked Debbie, and what had been a fairly cordial atmosphere suddenly turned chilly.

Debbie looked at Cass. 'You're the one who's friendly with the policeman. Do you know anything?'

Emma and Colin both turned to look at her, and Cass felt her face grow hot. 'I'm sure I don't know any more than you. The inspector has interviewed me and my fingerprints have been taken. I was the prime suspect for a while. But he doesn't discuss police matters with me.'

'Prime suspect?' Colin leaned forward in his seat. 'Is this a murder investigation? I thought Dad fell in the pool because he was drunk.' He looked accusingly at Debbie. 'That's what you told me.'

'I didn't say Michael was drunk, just that he'd been drinking. There was a bottle of wine on the table by the pool.'

'But that's what you were hinting at. He has a glass of wine occasionally, that's all. If he really was drunk, then I reckon someone drove him to it.'

'Don't start, Colin,' Emma said mildly. 'Whatever happened, the police will find out.'

'But you said you were a prime suspect, Cass. Do the police think Dad was murdered?'

Cass wished he'd stop putting words in her mouth. 'The police said there were a few loose ends, that's all. As far as I know they suspect everyone until a case is closed. I was right there at the scene — I found Michael in the pool, so I had to be a suspect.'

'Leave her alone, Colin.' Emma gave Cass a sympathetic look. 'It must have been awful for you.'

'Not nearly as awful as it was for me,' Debbie interrupted. 'I came back from London to find my husband dead and some strange woman in my house being questioned by the police. I didn't know what to think.'

'How much you'd just inherited, probably.' Colin stood up. 'I'm going for a walk. I'm sorry, Cass. Perhaps we can get together later.' He left the room without waiting for a reply.

Cass stood up. 'I ought to go, as well. I don't like leaving my mother alone for too long. Thank you for asking me over, Debbie.' She hesitated. 'My mother asked if you would like to come to our house and meet her sometime.'

'Oh, that would be really nice,' Debbie said enthusiastically. 'I'd love to meet your mother. Shall I invite her over here so she can see the house Michael built?'

Cass shook her head. 'Dora doesn't go out; she suffers from a mild form of agoraphobia. But she said to tell you you're welcome anytime.' Which wasn't quite true, but it was Dora's suggestion, so she could suffer the consequences.

'You go, Cass,' Emma said. 'Give Dora our love. If we get a chance we'll come and visit before we leave.'

Glad of an excuse to get out of the house, Cass thanked Debbie again and left with as much haste as she could without looking rude. She worried for a minute or two about Emma, but Emma was used to her brother's mood swings, and she was a good enough actress to pretend she actually liked her step-mother.

On the drive back Cass decided the afternoon could have been worse. Colin had deliberately baited Debbie, but it didn't seem to bother her too much. Maybe ignoring him was the best way to deal with his rudeness. She would bear that in mind in future.

She walked in the back door to find Liz sitting at the table with her mother. Liz gave her a sympathetic look.

'That bad?'

Cass dropped her bag on the floor

and sat down at the table with them. She took the mug of tea her mother handed her. 'Not as bad as I expected, but not good. Debbie did try to be nice, but Colin was being his usual awkward self.'

'How's Emma? The poor child has always played piggy-in-the-middle. Colin was always a bit of a problem. He didn't really get on with his father, either.'

'Emma's hardly a child, Mother. She's all grown up now and well able to look after herself.' Cass picked up her bag with a sigh. 'I've got to check the necklace over and see if I left any bits of wire sticking out. When Debbie tried it on, she said it hurt her.'

Dora leant across the table. 'Let me have a look at it, Cassie. How did it hurt her?' Cass tipped the necklace out of its bag Dora picked it up. 'Did it burn her?'

Cass could cheerfully have killed her mother. Dora always had to turn something simple into a major super-natural event. She had no idea how her

148

mother knew the mark on Debbie had looked like a burn, but she knew there was a logical explanation. Maybe rubies were known for their heat retention. 'She had a red mark on her chest where the stone had rested but the stone couldn't have got hot enough to mark her, so I'm pretty sure it was caused by a piece of the gold wire.'

'No, you're not,' Dora said crossly. 'I'm always telling you to open your mind. The woman had a burn mark on her neck, didn't she? Not a scratch a piece of wire would make. You don't believe in anything unless it jumps out and bites you, Cassie — and now it has.'

'The stone was in a beam of sunlight just before Debbie tried the necklace on,' Cass said stubbornly. 'I suppose the stone might have heated up enough to make a pink mark, but it wasn't a proper burn.'

'Did Debbie say the stone felt hot?'

Cass wanted to lie, but what was the point? 'She said it felt a little warm, which was understandable since it had been in the sun.'

Dora gave her daughter a sympathetic look. 'I know you don't want to believe, but you have a gift, Cassie. You give life to your stones.'

Liz reached for the pendant. 'This is the first time I've seen it finished. It really is beautiful, isn't it? May I try it on? We'll see if it scratches me.'

The necklace hung a little lower on Liz, nestling comfortably between her breasts. 'It feels warm,' she said, 'but pleasantly so. About blood temperature, I should think.'

'It doesn't glow on you as much as it did on Emma. But the ruby is Emma's birthstone.'

'Isn't it Debbie's birthstone as well? It should have been just right for her.'

Cass knew that perfectly well. She didn't have to be reminded. She just wanted to make good jewellery that suited the client. She didn't want the damned stones coming to life and making their own decisions. They were supposed to do what they were told.

'Why would my ruby would burn someone?' she asked, more to humour her mother than anything else. 'Did it take a dislike to Debbie? Or was it trying to do me out of my thousand pounds?'

Dora ignored the questions. 'Did you ask Michael's wife to come and visit?'

'Yes, I did, and she said she would. I don't think Michael told her about your affair. She seemed quite eager to meet you.'

'Oh, I'm sure he told his new wife all about me. If Michael was going to marry someone, he wouldn't keep any secrets from her.' Dora smiled. 'I'm really looking forward to meeting the new Mrs Lansdale.'

8

Noel put up a murder board. Not just to please Kevin, but because he thought it might help him sort out the pieces of his puzzle. Maybe it would point to some sort of pattern, or give him a clue what to do next. He knew a piece of the puzzle was missing. Most likely the cornerstone. According to the encyclopaedia on his desk, a cornerstone is the first stone set in the construction of a foundation. It is vitally important because it determines the position of the entire structure. Without that missing piece, nothing will hold together.

At the moment he was just collecting more puzzle pieces that didn't fit anywhere.

He had sent Kevin to the Lansdale house to pick up any pictures he could of Michael Lansdale, and Kevin had come back with just three. There was a photograph of Debbie on her own, one of Michael on his own, and one of the couple together. In the last one Michael had his arm draped casually across Debbie's shoulders. All three pictures had been taken in Spain, possibly on Michael's cabin cruiser, and now they adorned the murder board. He peered at the picture of Debbie and Michael together. That photo had definitely been taken on a boat. He could see the rail and part of the deck, so someone else had been on Michael's boat at the time the picture was taken. He noticed Debbie wasn't wearing her diamond engagement ring in the picture, and made a note to ask her about that.

He walked away from the board and sat down at his desk, opening the folder that held Debbie Lansdale's statement. He had studied the information until he knew it by heart, but there was nothing out of the ordinary. He was about to shut the file when something stopped him. Kevin had written down the times of the trains, both to and from London, and Brenda had spoken to the Harley Street clinic. He had also interviewed Debbie Lansdale twice himself. He flipped the A4 pages again. Something was off.

He picked up a pen and wrote down the time Debbie said she left the clinic. Then he checked the time the train left London and the time it arrived at Mickford station. His own report gave the exact time Debbie had turned up at the house, and the moment she saw Michael being loaded into an ambulance and had her little fit of hysterics. What no one had bothered to check was how long the drive from the station to the house would normally take. Noel looked at the figures in front of him. The distance from the railway station to the Lansdales' house was about eight miles. Debbie would have to check the car out of the station car park but, even allowing for traffic, the journey wouldn't take an hour and a half. Maybe she'd stopped off to pick something up on her way home, but if so she had she hadn't mentioned it. He was pretty sure he'd asked whether she'd driven straight home, and she'd told him she had.

He wrote JOURNEY TIME on a white card and added a big red question mark, then he pinned the card to the board. He had a feeling there would be a few more red question marks before he solved the case.

He still had no logical reason to suspect Debbie Lansdale, apart from the fact that her husband had left her a large amount of money in his will, as well as the house and the boat. Maybe he should seriously consider Cassandra Moon as a suspect, but she had no motive that he could discover. If she'd wanted Lansdale dead, she could have asked her mother to put a spell on him.

He was still smiling to himself when Brenda wandered into the room. She looked at the open file on his desk. 'Found anything?'

'Some extra time that can't be accounted for, but I'm sure Mrs Lansdale will have a perfectly plausible explanation as to why it took her well over an hour to drive the short distance from the railway station.'

'And it's not particularly important, is it? We know she wasn't at the house the time her husband was killed. She was either still in London or on her way home.' Brenda patted his hand. 'Never mind, it will all come together in the end, and I still think it's a good idea to pay a visit to the clinic in London. If there's anything funny going on, you won't find out over the telephone. If you still want to do that yourself, I'm sure one of our female police officers would be delighted to act as your wife or girlfriend.'

He looked thoughtful for a few seconds and then grinned at her. 'Leave it with me for the moment; I've just had a better idea.'

* * *

Cass was bored. Liz had worked three long days in a row, with no time left to go out in the evening, and her mother had developed a taste for reality shows on TV. She had checked the ruby necklace for random bits of wire and found none. She almost wished she had found something to explain the mark on Debbie's neck. The only logical explanation was the stone heating up when the ray of sunlight caught it. It was a crystal, after all, but she had never come across that phenomenon before.

When the phone rang she was sure she was going to hear Debbie's voice. The burn had probably become septic and she was about to be sued. She grabbed the receiver in her studio before Dora had a chance to pick up in the house.

'I'm sorry to bother you, Cass,' Debbie said. 'But Colin and Emma are talking about coming to see your mother tomorrow and I wondered if I could tag along. Please say if you'd rather I didn't.'

Why do people say things like that?

Cass wondered. She could hardly say, 'I'd rather you didn't,' not without a good reason, and she couldn't think of one right now.

'We'd love to see you,' she said, hoping the woman wouldn't cotton on to the fact that she was lying through her teeth. 'My mother has already asked me to invite you over.' At least that wasn't a lie. 'By the way, I've checked your necklace, and I can't find any stray wire or anything else that could hurt you, so you can take it back with you.'

'Thank you. I'll make sure I keep it out of the sun.'

Cass thought she detected a hint of sarcasm in that last sentence but it was difficult to tell over the phone. She pushed the button to end the call and went into the main house to tell her mother they were having visitors.

'I'd rather face her on her own,' Dora said, 'but I want to see Michael's children again. It's been years. I think the last time they came here Emma had just graduated from university. Tell me what Michael's wife looks like again, so I know what to expect. Is she pretty?'

'I wouldn't call her pretty; she's got a hard look about her. But she dresses well, better than I thought she would.' Cass smiled. 'I was trying to visualise how a barmaid in Marbella would dress, and I got it all wrong. She's blond, average height, and her eyes are a rather intense blue. I thought she might be wearing contacts at first, but maybe not, and she's slimmer than I imagined. We both expected Michael to send a picture of her, didn't we? Either by email or phone, but he said he wanted to keep her as a surprise.'

'Stupid man,' Dora muttered.

'You shouldn't have sent him away,' Cass said quietly. 'He was devastated when you wouldn't marry him.'

'I couldn't marry him.'

'Why not? I know you liked him. If you'd married him he wouldn't have gone to Spain and met Debbie.' Cass stopped herself before she said any more. It wasn't her mother's fault

Michael had died.

'I couldn't save him, Cassie. Even if I'd married him, he would still have met her and died. I may be a witch, but I can't change fate.' She gave Cass a small, sad smile. 'And I couldn't marry Michael because, legally, I'm still married to your father.'

'But you said . . . ' Cass started the sentence but had to stop because her vocal cords had seized up. The news was so astonishing she could hardly breathe, let alone speak. Her mother had never said anything about a husband. Cass had always assumed she was the result of a moment's silliness. Something her mother didn't want to talk about. Michael had been around for as long as she could remember and she had no recollection of any other men in her mother's life. Now, suddenly, she had a father.

'Is he still alive?'

She said it angrily, because she felt angry, but most of the anger was directed at herself. Why had she never asked?

Not one single question since the day she started to talk. Always happy to let it be. And now she discovered he might be out there somewhere. A proper father. Someone who was married to her mother.

Dora was staring at the stove where yet another pot sent up a haze of pungent vapour. 'I don't know, Cassie. Not for sure. He was alive a year ago, but he never stays in one place for long.' She turned to look at Cass, her eyes full of emotion. 'I should have said something years ago, but I didn't tell you because you never asked.'

And there it was. She had never asked because her father had never cared enough to come and find her. 'Does he know about me?' she asked softly.

Dora nodded, and it was only then that Cass noticed the trail of a tear down her mother's cheek. 'Of course he knows about you. But he's a dangerous man, Cassie. We both thought it best if he stayed away from you.'

'Shouldn't I get a say in that? How

is he dangerous? Is he a criminal? A murderer or something?' Cass couldn't believe she was approaching thirty and had only just found out she had a father. A father who had deliberately stayed away from her since the day she was born. No wonder she had been a strange child. No wonder her stones burned people and her mother couldn't leave the house. 'Do you know where he is?'

'I have no idea. I don't know if he's alive or dead. I only hear from him occasionally — and he always asks about you.'

Was she supposed to get excited about that? She wanted to wipe the tear from her mother's face, but she couldn't move. She felt betrayed, and also guilty and a little scared. 'Why is he dangerous? Is he in prison? Is that why he's not around?'

'No.' Dora tucked a strand of silver hair behind her ear and wiped a hand across her face. The tear stain was gone and the moment of vulnerability had passed. 'No, he's not a criminal. He's a warlock.'

Cass sighed. Not that again. If her mother felt cornered, she used the same old magic trick. Everyone in the family was a witch or a wizard. That was supposed to explain everything. *What's the difference between a wizard and a warlock?* she wondered. Not that it mattered. She certainly wasn't going to ask.

She got up from the table and headed for the door. 'If he contacts you again, tell him I want to speak to him.' As she passed her mother she gave the little witch a quick hug. 'Don't worry about it, Mum. I'm not going to.'

That got a smile from Dora. 'You never call me Mum.'

'I just did,' Cass said. 'But I probably won't do it again, so make the most of it.'

She headed for her studio. She needed time on her own, some time to think, and wonder why she had never asked those questions before. Part of the problem was that Dora never seemed able to answer a question like a normal person. The answer always involved witchcraft in some way. It was her mother's escape route. An easy way out of every dilemma.

Cass saw the ruby necklace lying on her desk and shook her head in disgust. Now she was forgetting to lock away a valuable piece of jewellery. She held the pendant in the palm of her hand. Dora was right; the stone did have a life of its own. Cass looked at the ruby more closely. In the light from the window it looked as if it was pulsating, like a beating heart, but she knew that wasn't possible. The light was playing tricks again. She put the necklace back in the bag and locked it in her safe, leaving it to pulsate on its own in the dark.

She was feeling particularly nervy and unsettled, so the knock on her door made her jump. The person outside was either Liz or Noel Raven. They were the only ones who knocked on her door. She hoped it wasn't Noel, because she really wasn't in the mood for his sarcasm right now.

He must have interpreted her expression quite well, because he gave her a rueful grin. 'You're obviously pleased to see me. I can tell by the look on your face.'

She sighed. 'You might as well come in.'

'Also extremely gracious.'

'Look, I don't know why you're here, but this is not a good time. I'm feeling particularly grumpy at the moment.'

She was blocking the doorway, but he managed to edge past her. 'Why change the habits of a lifetime? May I ask what's making you particularly grumpy?'

She felt like hitting him, but instead she got two bottles of beer from the fridge and handed him one. 'If you're here in an official capacity you don't have to drink the beer. I can easily handle two by myself.'

He sat in her only comfy chair and popped the beer cap with his thumb. 'Something serious, then?'

165

'I've just found out I've got a father.'

He shook his head sympathetically. 'These things happen.'

Cass drank half her beer in one go, debating whether to throw the bottle at him. Her swivel chair was the only seating option left, so she sat in it and swivelled to face him. 'Why are you here, Noel?'

'I was going to ask you a favour, actually, but like you said, this may not be a good time. Tell me about the father thing. Has yours just turned up out of the blue? How come you didn't know about him?'

'Probably because I didn't ask. Probably because I don't want to know about him. And probably because I'm happy as I am, and don't need any more complications in my life.'

'All very good reasons. My family life is pretty complicated, so I know how you feel.'

'What was the favour you were going to ask?'

'I've decided to visit the Harley

Street clinic and speak to the cosmetic surgeon Mrs Lansdale is using as an alibi, but if I go in an official capacity no one will talk to me. Everything at the clinic is highly confidential — for obvious reasons.'

'So you're going on an undercover mission and you need a woman with you. Why don't you take a police woman?'

He shook his head. 'I already asked Brenda, and that was a big mistake.'

Cass visualised the small, plump police detective. 'She hardly needs anything enhancing.'

'That's what she told me.'

'And you think I do?' She liked watching him squirm. He kept his eyes firmly on her face, and she had to admire his control.

'No, that's not what I said. I believe lots of women — women who are already perfectly adequately endowed — still decide to have surgery. I wasn't suggesting for a moment that you . . . that you're not . . . Oh hell, Cass, help me out here.'

She laughed, and realised he had made her feel better without even trying. 'Are we going as girlfriend and boyfriend, or husband and wife?'

He looked startled for a moment. 'I hadn't thought that far ahead. I didn't think you'd agree to come with me.'

'Whyever not? I'd love to prick that alibi balloon of hers; and, besides, it should be a fun day out. I'm not going to strip off in front of you, though.'

'The thought hadn't entered my head.' He paused. 'But now it has. So, changing the subject, are you free tomorrow?'

Cass remembered Debbie's phone call. 'No, sorry. We have visitors tomorrow. Both the Lansdale children, *and* their stepmother.'

'Wow.' Noel looked impressed. 'Does your mother know? I thought she and Lansdale had a thing going at one time.'

'He asked her to marry him. She said no, and I didn't know why at the time, but it was because she was still married to my father. Still is, as far as I know.' She didn't want to talk about that any more right now, so she swung her chair round and looked at a calendar on the wall. 'I forget what day it is sometimes. I'm free at the end of this week. How about Thursday?'

'That should be fine. I'll look forward to it.'

He stood up, smiling at her, and she scrambled quickly to her feet. Having him looking down at her was disconcerting. He was too darned attractive, that was the problem. His hair was a bit too long, his jeans a bit too tight, and his smile a bit too cute, but otherwise there wasn't much to complain about. She'd started off disliking him intensely, but now she'd got to know him . . . She opened her front door and stood back. She didn't want to get too close to him right this minute. Her heart was racing for some reason and her breathing had become laboured. She met his eyes — and wished she hadn't. It would be all too easy to get lost in those pools of liquid silver. He reached out a hand to touch her and she felt a jolt of electricity. She was sure she saw a spark.

He drew his hand back. 'What just happened?'

She shook her head, incapable of speech. 'I don't know.' She rubbed her bare arms where the little golden hairs were standing on end. It felt stormy, with rain not far away, so it was possible that atmospheric pressure had caused a build-up of static, but something was going on.

The detective reached for her again and she moved quickly away from him. 'Please, Noel, just go. I think . . . ' She fumbled for words. 'I think you might hurt me if you touch me right now. I'll see you on Thursday.' She would have pushed him out of the door, but she dare not touch him. The thought of touching him sent hot blood racing crazily through her veins. She stood looking at him, imagining the feel of his skin beneath her hands, his arms around her waist, his mouth on hers . . . and that was the last thing she remembered.

Someone was slapping her face. Not hard — but persistently. She tried to tell them to stop, but she was pretty sure nothing coherent came out of her mouth.

'Can you hear me, Cass?'

She sat up groggily, trying to remember what had just happened. Did she faint? She never fainted.

'What's the last thing you remember?' Noel asked, a hint of worry in his voice.

Even in her present confused state she knew one thing for certain. She could never tell him the last thing she remembered. She had no idea where those thoughts had come from. She didn't even fancy him — not much, anyway. Definitely not enough to make her have an attack of the vapours.

'Static,' she said, trying to sound convincing. 'Something strange in the atmosphere, like before a storm. I often

171

get a headache before a storm.'

'That was more than a headache. You passed out cold. If I hadn't caught you, you would have hit your head on the floor. I felt it too, though. More magnetic than static. I needed to touch you.' He saw the look on her face and shook his head. 'Sorry, but that was how it felt. As if I needed to ground a magnetic field.' He rested his hand lightly on her bare arm. 'See? It's gone now.'

Cass wasn't sure whether to be glad or sorry. She would always wonder what would have happened if he had touched her when that electricity was still sizzling in the air. She had a feeling it would have been something neither of them would ever forget. She shook her head to clear it.

'I'm fine.'

'I'm taking you into the house. You need one of your mother's potions.'

Cass shuddered. 'No, thank you. A couple of aspirin will do.' She let him take her arm and lead her into the house where Dora was waiting for them.

Dora didn't ask what had happened. She sat Cass in a chair and poured pink liquid into a glass. 'Drink this, and I don't want any arguments.'

'She fainted,' Noel said.

Dora shook her head. 'No, she didn't. It knocked her out because she tried to fight it. It's my fault. I've been trying to keep her safe instead of warning her.'

Cass wondered why her mother always had to talk in riddles. She sniffed the glass and pulled a face. 'What the hell is this? I'm not drinking some herby thing when I don't even know what's in it.'

'Do what your mother tells you,' Noel said. 'Or I'll hold your nose and pour it down you.'

Dora snorted out a laugh. 'She'll drink it. Whatever happened, I think it scared her, and Cassie doesn't scare easily.'

'Stop talking about me as if I'm not

here.' Cass downed the contents of the glass. It tasted of strawberries and celery and wasn't as bad as she had expected. 'There, see? No nose-holding required.' She couldn't imagine how it would help but, actually, the potion did make her feel better. A warm glow gently worked its way round her body, slowing her heartbeat and relaxing her muscles. She felt her eyelids start to droop, and looked at her mother suspiciously. 'What was in that stuff?'

'Something to send you to sleep. Go and have a lie down.'

Noel laughed. 'You can't fight a good spell, Cass. I must go. I'll see you on Thursday.'

Cass waited until Dora had closed the door behind Noel and then glared at her mother. 'You know what happened to me, don't you? Why I blacked out?'

'I have some idea what might have happened.' Dora's smile was smug. 'But you won't be able to stay awake long enough to hear my thoughts on the matter, so you might as well go and lie down before you fall down. The spell will be gone by dinnertime.'

She hadn't the energy to argue. She crawled upstairs to her room and lay on her bed, letting sleep take her. Tomorrow, Debbie Lansdale and Pandora Moon would meet face to face. As she started the dreamy slide into sleep, she wondered why she was imagining a battle between the gods of good and evil.

9

A summer storm, the weather people called it, caused by the exceptionally hot weather the country had been having lately. By lunchtime, dark clouds had gathered overhead and there was a rumble of thunder in the distance.

Cass could feel the electricity in the air. Her headache was back, and she half-expected to see sparks flying from her fingertips. She tried applying fresh makeup after her third shower of the day, but her lipstick felt greasy and even a light dusting of powder stuck to her skin in uneven lumps. She gave up, and settled for an extra lick of mascara instead. After studying herself in the mirror, she decided indigo jeans and a pale blue tank top went quite well with the fresh, unmade-up look. There was no point in over-dressing in this heat, even though she was sure Debbie

Lansdale would look perfectly groomed whatever the weather.

When Cass walked into the kitchen, Dora was wearing her usual caftan. This one was black silk dotted with silver stars and crescent moons. It covered her in softly draped folds from her neck to her ankles, but it still managed to look surprisingly sexy. She was standing over a pot of something that looked like wilted spinach leaves, stirring the mess with a wooden spoon.

'All you need is a pointy hat.'

Dora looked up from her pot. 'Wouldn't that be overdoing it a little?'

Cass laughed. She knew Dora's choice of clothes was quite deliberate. Her mother was already known as a witch on the internet, so why not live up to the image? 'Do you need the stove on?' she asked. 'It's hot enough already.'

'Not in here. The air conditioning is keeping everywhere cool.'

They didn't have air conditioning, but Dora was right. The kitchen was nice and cool. Cass sighed. This was the reason she had grown up not asking questions. The answers were always too unsettling.

'Are we giving them tea?'

'Of course.' Dora rinsed her hands and wiped them on a cloth. 'I've set everything out in the dining room.'

'The dining room?' Cass's voice rose with surprise. Her mother hated the dining room, so it was never used. 'You don't like the dining room.'

'Yes, I do. It's a lovely room. A bit claustrophobic sometimes, but I've opened the doors into the garden. There are roses right outside, so everything smells lovely, and I've put out the best china and napkins. I found a tin of biscuits left over from Christmas that we've never opened. Come and see.'

The room looked quite different. Instead of the dark, rather gloomy place Cass remembered, the large room was filled with sunlight and the smell of flowers. Dora had spread a lace cloth over the small oval table and set out the best china. The pink velvet of a little sofa Cass had forgotten all about shone with a soft lustre, and the Victorian fireplace now held an assortment of candles. The storm clouds were still hovering overhead, but without covering the sun, and Cass wondered for a moment if her mother could control the weather. She seemed to be able to do most things.

'It's going to rain in a little while.'

Dora tutted. 'Don't be a party pooper, Cassie. I'm waiting for you to tell me the room looks nice.'

'Yes, it does. It looks very nice. I'm sorry if I seem unappreciative, but I'm worried about this afternoon. You're going to do your witch thing, aren't you? Why can't you be a normal person for once?'

'Like her? Like the new Mrs Lansdale? She's not normal, Cassie. Even Noel knows that. He thinks she killed Michael. That's why I need to meet her. There's something very wrong happening, something evil, and I need to know what it is before anyone else gets badly hurt.'

Cass wiped a hand across her face. The room was almost too cool, but she was still sweating. 'What if Debbie did do it? What if she really did murder Michael? What are you going to do about it? If she thinks for one moment you've found her out, she's going to be coming after you.'

Dora smiled. 'If she does, I'll be ready for her. Help me put these chocolate biscuits on a plate.'

Cass twitched when she heard a knock on the front door, but after a hopeful look at her mother that got absolutely no response, she opened the door herself.

The three of them stood outside in a triangle — Colin in front with Emma slightly behind him, Debbie bringing up the rear. Colin and Emma looked nervous, but Debbie had a look of anticipation in her bright blue eyes. Emma was wearing stonewashed jeans and a skinny top, almost a mirror image of Cass, but Debbie had gone all out with the chic look; a short black skirt teamed with a silky yellow shirt, and stiletto sandals. Cass half-hoped her mother's fictitious air conditioning packed up. Yellow was a beast of a colour if you started to sweat.

A rumble of thunder had Cass ushering them all inside the house and through to the dining room. The scent of roses gave a delicate background note to the smell of freshly baked cinnamon buns that Dora hadn't thought to mention. Here the little witch was on her home territory, and although she was several inches shorter than Debbie her aura of power was almost visible.

Emma rushed to Dora and gave her a hug. 'I haven't seen you for ages, Aunty Dora. I've followed you on Twitter, though. You must be doing quite well with your potions, even though you don't charge enough.'

Colin bent down to kiss Dora on the

cheek, and then decided to do the introductions himself. 'This is Debbie,' he said. 'She married our father and now she owns the house he built. Debbie, this is Dora, our father's mistress.'

Cass wondered if it would look rude to run and hide in her studio. The trouble had started already and they hadn't even poured the tea. She reached for the plate of biscuits, thinking if everyone had their mouths full they might shut up, but Dora was holding out her hand to Debbie.

'It's so nice to meet you at last.' She gave Colin a reproving look, and Cass waited for him to turn into a mouse. 'My affair with Michael was over a long time ago. When he died, I hadn't seen him for five years.'

Dora held Debbie's hand a little longer than necessary, and Cass could see the woman was dying to pull away. 'You have a lovely house,' Debbie said, rubbing her hand. 'But it's really tucked away, isn't it? It's a good job Emma was driving. I would never have found this place on my own.'

'No,' Dora said. 'You wouldn't.'

To say the atmosphere was strained would have been an understatement. What appeared to be small talk was actually a verbal battle. Cass and Emma tried to keep the conversation light, while Colin sulked silently in a corner of the room, refusing to enter into the discussion at all. It was probably a good thing, Cass decided, because he seemed incapable of anything except rudeness.

'How long have you lived here?' Debbie asked. 'The house must have a fascinating history. I'd love to take a look around.'

'The house does have a fascinating history. Perhaps we should open it to the general public.' Dora's smile didn't quite reach her eyes. 'When we do, I promise I'll let you know.'

Debbie got up and walked out on to the patio. Cass wasn't quite sure whether the woman was furious with Dora or just interested in the roses. At that moment a flash of lightning lit up the tiny patio, followed by a clap of thunder that rattled the windows.

'It's starting to rain,' Debbie said as she came back inside. 'Perhaps we had better go, Emma, before the storm gets worse.'

Dora shut one of the French doors, leaving the other one open. She looked quite pleased with herself, as if she had just accomplished something important, but Cass had no idea what that might be. As far as she was concerned, the afternoon had been exactly the disaster she had predicted.

Dora put a hand on her daughter's arm. 'You haven't given Debbie her necklace, Cassie. If it's quite finished, she can take it home with her.'

Cass felt her stomach tighten. There was no sunlight around, so the stone shouldn't get hot, but she still felt unreasonably anxious. She had checked several times for random pieces of wire, but had found nothing. 'I'll get it,' she said. 'It's in my studio.'

184

'Can I come with you?' Debbie asked. 'I'd love to see where you work.'

Cass saw her mother give a slight shake of her head. 'It won't take me a minute,' she said quickly. She didn't want Debbie prowling around her studio. The thought of Michael's wife loose in a room full of crystals brought her out in a sweat.

She unlocked the safe and took out the velvet bag, tipping the necklace onto the palm of her hand. The ruby glowed with light, the tiny diamonds glistened, and the pearls shone like dewdrops on the delicate gold leaves. Cass decided she had done the very best she could, and she hoped Michael liked it, wherever he might be.

As she walked back into the dining room everyone's eyes turned to her. Feeling like a conjurer about to pull a rabbit out of a hat, she slipped the necklace from the bag and held it up by the chain she had made from tiny gold beads. The ruby was still the centre of attention: a deep, dark red, smooth and beautiful. Cass remembered the burn mark on Debbie's neck and hoped the stone behaved itself. It seemed quiet now, almost docile, and Cass hoped it wasn't the lull before the storm.

'Do you want to wear it now? Or would you rather wait until your birthday?'

'I'll wear it straight away now it's finally finished.' Debbie looked at Cass. 'As long as you've checked for bits of stray wire.'

'Yes, I have.' Cass was holding her temper in check with difficulty. 'I looked at it through a loupe to be certain. There are no bits of stray wire.'

'I'll put it on for you, Debbie.' Emma took the necklace from Cass with a smile. 'To be honest, I just want a chance to hold it again. Perhaps you could make some earrings for my birthday, with tiny rubies. Something I can afford.'

'Of course I will.' Cass held her breath as Emma clasped the chain round her stepmother's neck, but nothing happened. There was a muted rumble of thunder in the distance as the storm moved away, and Cass felt as if some sort of disaster had been averted. It seemed she had been worrying for no reason.

Dora managed a fairly gracious goodbye. 'You must come again,' she said in a voice that told everyone she didn't mean a word of it. 'Ever since Michael told me he was getting married again, I've been looking forward to meeting you. You aren't a bit what I expected.'

Debbie stopped as she was about to go out of the door. 'I'm not a barmaid anymore, Mrs Moon. You should remember that.'

'Oh, I will.' Dora answered. 'I never for one moment thought of you as a barmaid.'

Debbie hesitated for a moment, as if she couldn't decide whether she had just been complimented or insulted, and then walked outside without a backward glance.

★   ★   ★

Noel was working on his murder board. He had grudgingly admitted it was a good idea and tacked a large piece of corkboard to the wall. Every clue and photograph was now pinned up where everyone could see it. He had let Kevin arrange the evidence in chronological order and now he could see where the pieces should go, even though he hadn't got all of them. He had managed to get photos of the principal players: Michael Lansdale, his new wife and his two children. He hadn't yet added Cassandra Moon to the board because he couldn't get hold of a photo of her. He had Googled her and got zilch. Perhaps he could ask Dora, but he wasn't sure of his reception. He didn't want Dora to think he had designs on her daughter. It might not be a good idea to get on the wrong side of Pandora Moon.

After studying the board for a few more minutes, he called Kevin and Brenda into the room. 'Deborah Lansdale is still our only real suspect,' he told them, 'and I refuse to write her off because she seems to have an unbreakable alibi. Kevin, I want you to make sure Mrs Lansdale was on the trains to and from London at the times she gave us. Go to the station tomorrow and speak to people who use the same trains Mrs Lansdale used. Take a picture with you and find out if anyone saw her. Also, check if there are any security cameras. We should have done that on the day of the murder, but better now than never. There should be at least one in the car park.'

'All that will do is confirm her alibi,' Brenda said. 'Then where are we?'

'No worse off and at least we'll have done a thorough job.' He turned away from the board. 'The woman in the taxi has disappeared, by the looks of it. A couple of officers did a thorough house-to-house. No one saw her or knows where she went, so we might as well write her off, and it looks as if we may never know what actually killed Michael Lansdale. He could have slipped and fallen into the pool all by himself, according to our resident pathologist, who now has a sore bottom from sitting on the fence; but it's more likely a lounger cushion stopped him breathing and someone dragged him into the water. There were no signs of a heart attack or stroke.'

Kevin walked over to peer at the board. 'That picture of Debbie Lansdale looks like a selfie.'

'What makes you think that?' Brenda asked in surprise.

'Because her face is too close to the camera. If someone takes a photo of you they usually stand back a bit.' Kevin pulled a mobile phone out of his pocket and held it at arm's length. After taking a photo of himself he held it out for them to see. 'My face is about the same distance away.'

Noel bent down to look at the screen. 'A fraction further away if anything, but I expect your arms are longer than hers.' He turned back to his board. 'Can you see that blurry bit in the bottom left corner of the photo? I bet that's her arm. She couldn't hold the camera far enough away to get a clean picture. That was a good call, Kevin. I hadn't spotted it.'

Kevin glowed with pride. 'Always glad to be of assistance, boss.'

Noel couldn't think what good that piece of information was at the moment, but it might be important later. He turned to Brenda. 'I want you to drive to the station and log the time it takes you to get back to the Lansdales' house. Do it in the late afternoon, as if you'd just got off the same London train as Debbie Lansdale.'

'I checked on her thoroughly,' Brenda said. 'She'd been working at the bar in Marbella for about six months. She was well liked by her workmates and the girl whose apartment she shared. She's got a clean police record, both here and in Spain. No living family members. And everyone was pleased when she met Michael Lansdale and they got married. Like a fairy story, her friends are quoted as saying.' She picked up her notebook and flipped over a page. 'Although there was one thing I noticed that was a bit odd. Lansdale didn't have any photos of his wife. Not in his wallet, and not at the house. The only photo of the two of them together is the one she gave to you. Maybe that's why she took a selfie. Perhaps they left some things in Spain, like photos and books and things, and they're getting them shipped over later.'

Noel frowned. 'Kevin can check that out, but doesn't every man carry a photo of his wife in his wallet? I thought it was compulsory.'

Brenda shook her head. 'Not in this day of mobile phones. Did anyone find Lansdale's phone, by the way?'

'Yes, at the bottom of the pool. We couldn't get it going again, not even after it was professionally dried out. Our expert said it looked like the sim card had been wiped clean, but he wouldn't swear to it, not when the phone had been in a swimming pool.'

'No one will swear to anything these days,' Brenda said with a sigh. 'The thought of standing up in court and actually having an opinion frightens them all to death. I'll check the train station on Thursday,' she told Noel.

'I'll be in London at the Harley Street clinic that day.'

'Who're you taking with you?'

'Cassandra Moon.' He frowned. 'What are you both grinning at? You wouldn't come with me, Brenda, so I had to find someone else.'

'Of course you did.' Brenda couldn't hide her smile. 'Kevin wouldn't have been much help, would he?'

'I could have implants in my pecs, I suppose. It would be easier than working out every day.'

'Is that what you do, Kev? Work out every day? If so, you should stop, because it's not working.'

Noel shooed them both out of his office and went back to studying the board, but his heart wasn't in it. He kept thinking of Cassandra Moon and the flash of electricity that had sparked between them. He had met women before who had excited him, but this had been different. More physical than sexual. A jolt to his whole body as if he'd touched a live wire, and the way she had kept him at arm's length afterwards suggested she had felt exactly the same thing. That interested him. He was quite looking forward to having her all to himself for a whole day. He might be able to find out a bit more about her — and her mother. Pandora Moon fascinated him. Looking into those jewel-coloured eyes, he could almost believe she really was a witch.

* * *

Cass said goodbye to Colin and Emma while Debbie went on ahead to unlock the car.

'The police are releasing the body tomorrow,' Emma said quietly. 'So Debbie can arrange the funeral. I think Daddy will be cremated because that's what she wants, and it's not worth making a fuss.'

'I don't agree; I think we should make a fuss,' Colin grumbled. 'But I'm outnumbered, as usual. She's determined to get him on the funeral pyre as soon as possible, regardless of what we think.' He looked at Cass reproachfully. 'I thought Dora would be on my side.'

He hadn't attempted to lower his voice and Debbie could probably hear every word he said. Cass didn't want to get involved in a family row. Michael was dead, and what happened to him next wouldn't change that. She hung back until they were out of Debbie's hearing range.

'My mother doesn't get to have a say in it either, Colin, and I'm inclined to agree with Emma. Why would Debbie say Michael had changed his mind if he hadn't? You could be going against his wishes by insisting on a funeral. None of us really know what happened in Spain, because we weren't there.'

They caught up with Debbie and she opened the passenger door. Colin deliberately climbed in the back, but

Emma joined her stepmother in the front of the car.

'Thank you for letting me meet your mother. She's an interesting woman.' Debbie put her hand on Cass's arm. 'I'll be in touch as soon as we have a date for the funeral. I'd like both of you to come back to the house afterwards. Just for a cup of tea.'

'Dora won't be able to come to the funeral; she doesn't leave the house. But I'll be there.'

'We can stay an extra night, if you like.' Emma glared at Colin as he kicked her on the ankle. 'We don't need to rush away.'

'Thank you.' Debbie gave her step-daughter a grateful smile. 'Thank you, Emma. But I'll be fine. I have to get used to living on my own. Just be there for me when I need you. That will make me feel a lot better.'

Colin rolled down the car window. 'See you in a couple of days, Cass, and give my love to Dora. I'd forgotten how much I miss her.'

Cass watched them drive away and then walked back inside. The storm had moved away and the air smelled clean and fresh. Dora was stacking plates and cups in the dishwasher.

'That was interesting,' she said over the clink of china. 'Informative, as well.'

Cass dropped into a chair. 'I'm just glad it's over. I don't want to go through that again for a while. And you were no help, Mother. You were deliberately trying to antagonise her.'

'Emotion is usually a good indication of a person's character, but not in Debbie's case. All her emotions are fabricated because she's empty inside. She doesn't have any emotion of her own. She's a fake.' Dora shut the door of the dishwasher with a little more force than necessary. 'I'm surprised Michael didn't see through her. He was an intelligent man, but I think she's a very clever woman. She must have been clever to take him in.'

'Michael fell in love with her, and we all know love is blind. He didn't look too closely because he wanted to believe she was perfect.' Cass took a deep breath. 'Did she do it, Mother? Did she kill Michael?'

'I think you already know the answer to that, Cassie, and so does Noel Raven. But she can only be defeated if you work together. On your own neither one of you is strong enough, and that's why I worry about you. Make sure you don't underestimate her. She was born without any understanding of morality. A true sociopath.'

Cass knew her mother was talking nonsense; but even so, a small shiver ran down her spine. Noel might very well believe Debbie was guilty, but he had no way of proving it.

'I'm going to the Harley Street clinic with Noel tomorrow. He wants to break her alibi. But if she was actually at the clinic at the time of Michael's murder, she couldn't have killed him, could she?'

'It seems that way — but nothing is quite as it seems. She's built a room of mirrors to hide behind, and you will have to shatter them to see the truth.'

'Yeah, right,' Cass said with a sigh. Asking her mother a simple question was never going to get a simple answer. 'She says she wants you to come to the funeral.'

'I can't, and she knows that. She doesn't really want me there. She knows I can see what she really is.' Dora carefully folded the lace table-cloth and put it in the dresser drawer. 'Take care, Cassie. You and Noel are getting close to the truth, and that might frighten her into doing something stupid. Something that could harm you.'

Surely stupid was better than clever, Cass thought, as she got ready for bed. Noel was a clever detective, and she was pretty damn clever herself some-times. The answer must lie at the clinic — Debbie either had been there or she hadn't — and tomorrow they would find out one way or the other.

10

Noel couldn't get away from his office until the afternoon, so Cass had lunch with Liz. She wanted to get a few pointers as to how to behave at the clinic. It had never occurred to her to have cosmetic surgery. Dora looked pretty good for her age, and Cass hoped her mother's genes had been passed on to her. She had no idea what sort of genes she might have inherited from her father because, as far as Dora was concerned, it was not the right time to go into details. Not while there were so many other things going on. She wouldn't even tell Cass his name.

Liz ordered her usual salad and Cass decided to have the same. Her stomach was giving little jumps every now and again, and she wasn't sure whether it was the thought of going to see a Harley Street surgeon, or spending time alone with Noel. Even though she kept telling herself her fainting attack had nothing to do with the detective, she didn't want to have a funny turn on the train.

'It's OK to be nervous,' Liz said through a mouthful of rocket. 'Everyone who goes into any sort of a hospital is nervous, even if they're only visiting. Did your detective make an appointment?'

'He's not my detective, and no, he didn't make an appointment, because our visit is unofficial and supposedly spur-of-the-moment. He doesn't want anything on file. We shall say we were just passing, and called in to pick up a brochure. With a bit of luck I can chat to the receptionist or whatever, and see what I can find out.'

'What if the doctor has time on his hands and suggests he take a look at you right there and then? I've heard they draw on your boobs with a marker pen and take pictures of you in the nude.'

'No one is drawing on my boobs or getting me in the nude. And definitely not in the presence of Noel Raven.'

'Surely he wouldn't expect to watch you being examined?'

'He'd find it highly amusing, and as he's posing as my boyfriend he could probably get away with it. Don't worry; I have no intention of taking my clothes off for anyone.'

Liz pushed her empty plate away. 'Can I have chocolate cake, as I only had salad?' She pulled a face when Cass shook her head. 'If this Debbie person is involved in Michael's death, aren't you putting yourself in danger? I don't think Noel should have asked you to go along. You're not a detective.'

'Exactly. That's why it's off the books. What harm can there be? Debbie Lansdale isn't going back to the clinic. Since Michael's death she's changed her mind about having cosmetic surgery, and I'm just making a casual enquiry. Besides, if she targets anyone, it's going to be my mother. Colin introduced Dora as Michael's mistress.'

Liz laughed. 'Good old Colin. If I remember rightly, he never was one to sugar-coat the truth. What did Dora say?'

'She said it was all over a long time ago, which was fine, but then she spent the rest of the afternoon being awkward. Debbie wanted a tour of the house, and Dora said the only way that would happen was if we opened it to the public. To be fair, Debbie wanted a look at my studio, and I said no to that as well.' Cass sighed. 'I wish I knew why I don't like the woman. If I don't like someone, I usually have a reason.'

'I must meet her,' Liz said, 'although I'm not very good at judging a person's character. Last week I felt really sorry for a man who'd been beaten up by his next-door neighbour, but then I found out my patient had deliberately poisoned the man's goldfish. It was a feud that had been going on for years. Sometimes we judge without knowing all the facts.'

'And nothing is ever quite what it seems.' Cass had no idea why she said that. It sounded more like something her mother would say. 'I'd better go,' she told Liz. 'It's probably a criminal offence to keep a detective inspector waiting, and you need to get back to work and save a few more lives.'

*   *   *

Cass drove to the station slowly. She was early and she didn't want to appear eager. Ridiculously, she felt as if she were on a first date. She parked the car and looked around to make sure Noel wasn't already parked and watching her, then she got out her lip gloss, checked her mascara hadn't run, and pulled a comb through her hair. Extra perfume might be a step too far. She was annoyed that it mattered so much what she looked like. Noel had asked her to go with him because he couldn't get anyone else to go. He had no interest in her, no hidden agenda. He needed to confirm a suspect's alibi, and that was all this was. Nothing else.

So why was she so damned nervous? she wondered as she looked at her watch. And really cross because he was five minutes late?

A few seconds later he pulled up next to her. 'Did you think I'd stood you up?' he asked as he got out of the car. 'I got held up with a phone call just as I was leaving. We've got five minutes to get our tickets, so get a move on.'

She followed him while he paid for two return tickets, and then had to run up the stairs behind him because the train was drawing in. He found a couple of seats and let her sit down first, lowering his lengthy frame into the seat opposite. He spent so long staring at her that she was glad she'd had time to repair any damage to her makeup. Even so, his gaze was a little disconcerting.

'Have I got a smut on my face?'

'I was just thinking what an unusual colour your hair is. You don't get it from your mother, do you?'

'Actually, I do. My mother's hair turned pure white some years ago. She was my colour up until then.' Cass smiled. 'I call it amber, but I relate most things to my gemstones. I suppose it's just a sort of reddish-brown.'

'No, amber is about right. What made your mother's hair turn white?'

The question sounded innocuous enough, but he was a police detective and she had no intention of talking about her family. Dora fiercely defended her privacy, and Cass wasn't going to let anyone intrude upon her mother's private life, quite apart from the fact that upsetting Dora often proved to be unwise.

'What do you want me to say when we get to the clinic?' she asked.

He gave her a lazy smile. 'Well fielded. So no questions about your family. Fair enough. Getting back to the clinic, I suggest we play it by ear depending on who we speak to. You could say Debbie Lansdale is a friend and she recommended the clinic. That might get us the information we want. It would be great if we could speak to the same doctor, but I doubt that will happen.' He stretched his legs out and she had to move her feet out of his way. 'What I don't want to do is give anyone cause to suspect we have an ulterior motive. I don't want to lose my job, and in the end this could all be a waste of time.'

'So all you want to do is find out if Debbie was there at the time Michael fell in the pool. It will take us about an hour and a half to get to Oxford Street station, plus however long it takes to walk to the clinic. It would have taken Debbie the same time, plus her consultation, and then the same time getting back home.'

'Which would put her in the clear. We'll have to handle this carefully. Make sure it doesn't sound like an interrogation.'

'Look, I may not be one of your highly qualified police detectives, but I'm not stupid. In fact, it might be a good idea if you left the talking to me.

I'm the one having my boobs done.'

'Let's not get carried away here. The police finances won't run to cosmetic surgery, even in the cause of justice, so for the moment you're stuck with the ones you were given.' He lowered his eyes. 'And they look just fine to me.'

She changed the subject with as much finesse as she could manage. 'You said you wanted to know what happened yesterday. Well, it was a disaster, just as I predicted.'

Noel leant forward in his seat. 'That sounds interesting. What happened?'

'Colin started everything off by introducing my mother as Michael's mistress. That set the tone for the rest of the day. Then Debbie asked to see round the house and was informed our home wasn't open to the general public. That was my mother being hospitable. Then there was a damned great flash of lightning and a clap of thunder just as Debbie decided to go out on to the patio. A storm outside as well as inside.'

Noel didn't speak for a minute and Cass looked at him curiously. 'What?'

He shook his head. 'I was just thinking — electricity again. Thunder and lightning and sparks between us. All very strange, isn't it?'

'Now you're starting to sound like my mother. Every time there's a storm she thinks the end of the world is coming. Anyway, nobody had a fun time at the party. Debbie was being overly polite and my mother was being very rude. Like I said, the whole thing was a disaster.'

He grinned at her. 'I think it sounds like fun.'

The rest of the journey passed fairly quickly while they discussed ways to ask questions at the clinic that wouldn't cause suspicion. She had an unsettling feeling that Noel was going to leave everything to her. When she pointed out that she knew absolutely nothing about cosmetic surgery, he told her that was the whole point of the exercise and precisely why he had brought her along.

They got out at Oxford Street station and took the underpass, mingling with strolling sightseers and hurrying office workers.

'What's your favourite item of clothing?' Noel asked suddenly.

Cass looked at him in surprise. 'Shoes, probably, and handbags. Accessories, rather than clothes.'

'So if we take a short cut through the John Lewis store and I steer you away from shoes and bags, we might make it out the other side.'

'Can I look at shoes on the way back?' She was falling behind him again, trying to keep up with his long strides and wishing she hadn't worn heels.

'No, you can't. We need to time our journey back, including the car ride from the station to the Lansdales' house. There will be no time for shopping.'

He had to keep grabbing her arm as they walked through the store. Cass thought it was really unfair to take her to London and then march her past an amazing array of merchandise without giving her time to look. A short walk took them to Harley Street, and now Cass had the pleasure of hustling Noel as he paused to drool over a yellow Lamborghini.

'No time to stop and stare, Inspector. We're on a mission, remember?'

She thought how pretty the street was. Most of the tall, terraced houses had been converted to offices, a high percentage to do with some aspect of the medical profession, though some looked as if they might still be privately owned. All of them were beautifully kept, with window boxes and freshly painted railings, the cars parked in the narrow street emphasising the wealth of the area. She dragged Noel away from his inspection of a bright red Maserati to point out a discreet brass nameplate beside the front door of one of the houses.

'That's it?' Noel sounded surprised. 'I was expecting something more obvious.'

'What? Like a neon sign over the

door? A woman going in there wants to keep her visit as discreet as possible.' She took a deep breath. 'Here we go, then. The fact that I'm as nervous as hell is probably right in character.'

The front door led them into a square hallway. On the right was a pretty room with a small desk and a sign saying 'enquiries'. The rest of the room was taken up with an assortment of mismatched seating, most of it upholstered in flowered brocade. A water cooler with plastic cups stood just inside the door. Cass felt a little let down. She had Googled the clinic and knew what they charged for their services, so she had expected more.

One of the chairs was occupied by a young woman who gave them a tentative smile before going back to her copy of *The Lady*, and sitting on a small settee by the window was a middle-aged couple whispering together nervously. Cass was beginning to feel the urge to turn and run. For some reason she had expected a hospital environment, and this rather ordinary little room with its Victorian fireplace was making her feel like the impostor she was. There was no way they were going to pull this off. Noel would be drummed out of the police force and she would finish up in prison.

'Can I help you?'

The voice made her jump. She hadn't seen the receptionist come back into the room. For a moment her voice deserted her. Noel pinched her arm and she tried to get her head back in gear. This was ridiculous. It wasn't real. She wasn't here to have someone examine her and arrange a painful operation. It was all make-believe. The woman behind the desk looked like everyone's mother. Her hair was cut short and starting to go grey and her eyes were kind and understanding. She was wearing a pale blue blouse and a black cardigan, and Cass was sure she had sensible shoes on her feet, even though they were hidden behind the desk.

'I'm sorry,' Cass said, the quiver in

213

her voice unfeigned. 'I . . . we just wanted to make some enquiries.' She cleared her throat. 'A friend of mine was here recently and she said everyone was . . . er . . . very nice.' She looked at Noel for help, but he just smiled encouragingly. 'My friend's name is Debbie Lansdale. She was going to have an operation to . . . er . . . but her husband died, so I think she cancelled.'

'Oh, Mrs Lansdale. Of course I remember her. A lovely lady. So sad about her husband. She phoned to say she would have to put off her next appointment. My name's Sandra. Please give her my condolences when you see her.'

'I will,' Cass said, 'and thank you. She was here the day her husband died and she blames herself, thinking if she had been at home with him . . . you know?' Out of the corner of her eye Cass noticed that Noel had taken himself out of the way and was sitting in a chair reading a magazine.

'What date would that have been?'

Sandra was checking the computer screen on her desk. 'It was about ten days ago, wasn't it?'

'The third,' Cass said. 'I feel bad about just dropping in, but Debbie said I should make an appointment with you. She *was* here that day, then, was she?'

The receptionist looked up at her. 'Yes, in the afternoon. It was Mrs Lansdale's first consultation. She saw Mr Devon, our chief cosmetic consultant.'

Cass felt her heart sink. It looked as if Debbie's alibi was pretty solid. 'Would it be possible for me to have a quick word with Mr Devon? Debbie said he's absolutely brilliant, but this is a big deal for me, and I'd like to meet him before I make a decision.'

Sandra glanced across the room. 'If you wait with your friend, I'll see what I can do.'

'Thank you. I promise not to keep him more than a few minutes.' The woman was observant, Cass gave her that. The absence of a wedding ring must have given her away. She slid into a seat next to Noel. 'I'm seeing the consultant, Mr Devon, so I'll get the information right from the top man. I can't believe he'd be involved in a conspiracy with Debbie. Not in a place like this.'

Noel smiled. 'It's not what you expect, is it? Sort of shabby chic. They want people to know all the money is being spent on treatment rather than trivia. They use a private hospital here in London for the actual operations, so I expect that's where most of the money goes. And Mr Devon is top of his class as far as boob ops go. You'd be safe in his hands — figuratively speaking, of course.'

Cass was surprised how the scenery changed once she was led through a door into the inner sanctum. Now it was more clinical, with polished floors and pristine white walls. A very slight smell of antiseptic hung in the air, mixed with the heady perfume of lilac and freesia. The scent came from a vase of the flowers that stood in the corner of Mr Devon's large consulting room. The walls were covered with before-and-after photos, which she found a bit disconcerting. Mr Devon's hall of fame, no doubt.

Mr Devon wasn't what she had expected, either. All the consultants she had seen on television were tall, handsome men in their early sixties, with white highlights in their sideburns. The man in front of her was probably in his mid-forties, slightly rotund, with a large bald patch on top of his head. His jowls wobbled when he spoke and he certainly wasn't the best advertisement for cosmetic surgery. She had to remind herself he only dealt with a very specific part of a woman's anatomy. He waved her to a seat in front of a small antique desk and squeezed in behind it, lowering himself into an uncomfortable-looking swivel chair.

'You're a friend of Mrs Lansdale?'

'Yes, I am. Thank you for seeing me,

Mr Devon. Debbie asked me to tell you again how sorry she was to have to cancel, but you can understand . . . '

'Of course.' Mr Devon smiled and looked for a moment like a bald Father Christmas. 'She was only here for an initial consultation. Perhaps, once she is over her sad loss, she will come back. I am glad Mrs Lansdale recommended us. If you wish, you can make an appointment with my secretary on your way out. We can fit you in for a first consultation in about three weeks, and then there would be one more appointment before your operation. That is, if we both decide to go ahead. Sometimes an operation is unnecessary or too risky, and sometimes a woman will change her mind.'

'Thank you.' Cass got up from her chair. 'Debbie feels guilty for not getting home before her husband died, although I keep telling her she couldn't have got home any quicker. What time did she leave here? Do you remember?'

'Not offhand.' Mr Devon stayed in

218

his chair. 'But I always schedule an hour for a first consultation. I'm sure Mrs Lansdale has nothing to feel guilty about. She told me the augmentation was a gift from her husband. Something that would please them both. I'm sure he would have been happy she came to see me.'

Cass made her way back to Noel, trying to think of some way Debbie could have been in two places at once. She might have had an accomplice, but there was nothing so far to suggest anyone else was involved and, apart from a tenuous mention of a drug-dealing cartel in Spain, a suggestion made by Debbie herself, there were no other suspects.

Noel didn't say much on the way home in the train. She guessed he was disappointed in the outcome of their visit. Once they were in the car he looked at his watch.

'The train was right on schedule. I'll drive to the top of the lane that leads to the Lansdale's house and take a final time check. Even if Debbie Lansdale *was* at the clinic that day, *and* caught the train back, she certainly didn't drive straight home.' He looked at his watch again. 'There is still nearly an hour unaccounted for. We'll see what the traffic is like at this time of day.'

Cass sat beside him at the top of the narrow lane leading down to Michael's house. 'What was she doing in that hour? Not that it matters much. She couldn't have killed Michael. He was already dead by the time the train got into the station. She couldn't have done it, Noel. Her alibi is as tight as a sailor's knot.'

'Then who did do it?' He banged his fist on the steering wheel. 'I'm missing something. What was it your mother said — ? All is not what it seems. That's how I feel about this case. That missing piece of the jigsaw puzzle is close by; I just can't lay my hands on it at the moment.' He started the engine again. 'I'll take you home and have a word with your mother. She thinks the same way I do.'

Cass thought that was impossible. No one thought the same way as Dora. She had a thinking process all her own. 'I'll make you tea,' she told him. 'And my mother can make you a spell to help you find your killer.'

Dora met them at the front door, which was unusual to say the least. 'Is something wrong?'

Dora shook her head. 'I knew you were coming. I've put the kettle on and there are blueberry muffins in the oven.' She led them into the kitchen. 'I wish I could help you, Noel, but I can't. You have to work it out on your own.'

He threw his jacket over the back of a chair and sat down. 'Point me in the right direction, then.'

'There is no right direction. The lines of fate are infinite. Every time you make a decision you change the possible outcome.'

Cass found she could almost understand that. 'You said things are not what they seem. What did you mean?'

Dora smiled as she topped up mugs

with boiling water. 'Exactly what I said. You have to look at things differently to see the truth. What is it they say these days — ? Look outside the box? I don't know the answer, but you already have all the clues, so you should be able to work it out.'

'Please don't talk in riddles, Mother. This is too important. If you know anything, or if you've heard anything on the internet, you have to tell Noel.'

Dora handed round the mugs of tea. 'I've told you everything I know. Most of what you see is a mirage. You have to imagine the unimaginable.'

Cass threw up her hands. 'What's the point, Noel? She won't tell you anything sensible.'

'Wait a minute. What can't we imagine, Dora? How Debbie Lansdale killed her husband when she was miles away at the time? Did she do it? What haven't we thought of? An accomplice here in Mickford? A crooked Harley Street consultant? A drug baron from Spain?' He shook his head. 'I've considered every one of them. How about . . . I know! How about identical twins?'

Cass laughed. 'That would work, actually. It ticks all the boxes. It's the only way Debbie could be in two places at the same time. But, let's face it, it's highly unlikely.'

'Unimaginable?'

'You can't take what my mother says seriously, Noel. She lives in a different dimension.'

'Maybe that's where I need to go.' He put his mug on the table and stood up. 'Sherlock Holmes once said, 'When you have eliminated the impossible, whatever remains, however improbable, must be the truth.''

'You really believe Debbie has an identical twin sister?' Cass asked incredulously. 'You can't be serious!'

Noel slung his jacket over his shoulder. 'No, I don't believe that for a minute, but thank you, Dora. I asked you to point me in the right direction, and even though you couldn't do that, you've suggested I look in a different direction, and that may be all I need.'

Cass closed the door behind him and leant against it. She felt drained. The trip to London had been more stressful than she had expected, and all it had done was strengthen Debbie's alibi. She had been quite sure someone at the clinic was lying, or the records had been falsified, but Devon was a highly paid cosmetic consultant. Admittedly, Debbie had inherited a lot of money, but surely not enough to buy off someone like Devon. No, Noel was right. Something was staring them right in the face — they just couldn't see it.

11

It was late by the time Noel got back to his office, but Kevin and Brenda were still there, anxiously waiting for any leads he had picked up at the clinic. He shook his head at them.

'Not good. Debbie Lansdale was definitely at Harley Street when her husband was killed.'

Kevin looked crushed. 'So she's not a suspect anymore.'

'I didn't say that. I've decided the murders must have been committed by Debbie Lansdale's identical twin.'

'You're joking!' Brenda's eyes were enormous. 'She's got an identical twin?'

He laughed. 'No, she hasn't. At least I'm pretty sure she hasn't. But I'm also pretty sure she had a hand in her husband's death some way or another. Dora Moon says we have to think outside the box, look for something we wouldn't normally consider.'

Kevin pulled a face. 'The witch told you that? She's a bit nutty, you know. She sells magic spells on the internet.'

'Actually, she's a very clever lady. She makes a lot of money with her herbal remedies.'

Dora only sold the recipes for her concoctions on the internet, not the actual potions. Not that he cared. What she did wasn't illegal in any way. She had a team of school kids who collected weeds for her so she could experiment in her kitchen, and as long as it wasn't cannabis or anything dangerous it was none of his business. Cass and her mother both seemed quite comfortably off, and Noel wondered if Dora had a private income. Cass used precious stones in her jewellery, so someone had to be financing her.

Noel took off his jacket and sat behind his desk. 'So, what have you two come up with?'

'Not a lot.' Kevin opened his notebook. 'First off, I emailed the flatmate in Marbella. All the Lansdales' belongings have been shipped out. Neither of them left anything behind. Michael Lansdale had a designer furnish the house, so they only brought over some personal belongings. They wanted to start fresh, her flatmate said.' He turned a page. 'The coroner has released Mr Lansdale's body. I phoned Mrs Lansdale and informed her. I also asked her to let us know the date she arranges for her husband's cremation.' He flipped over another page. 'A body was found this morning at the bottom of Meg's Drop. I don't know how long it's been there, or who it is, but it seems unrelated to our case. It was the body of a female, so a woman out walking slipped and fell, most likely.'

'Anyone got a photo of the victim?'

Kevin shook his head. 'It wouldn't do you any good. The corpse was pretty messed up, evidently. Hit all those rocks and bushes on the way down. It's going to make identification difficult, but we should know a bit more by tomorrow.'

'So we don't know exactly how this person died?'

Kevin looked puzzled. 'She fell down a great big ravine.'

'What I meant was, did she fall or was she pushed? Did the fall kill her, or was she already dead before she went over the edge? We've had three deaths in less than three weeks, which is not exactly average for the area, so forgive me if I'm a bit suspicious.'

'Bad things always come in threes,' Brenda offered brightly. 'Good old storybook stuff.'

'No one's made a missing person report,' Kevin said, 'and if the woman has been down there a couple of weeks you'd think someone would have missed her by now. It would be easier if we had a name.'

'I'll go and have a look at the site of the accident tomorrow if I can find the time. No point in going now; it's almost dark. I presume the body has been removed and the area cordoned off?'

Kevin nodded. 'Yellow tape and

bollards, so no one tries to look down. It's a long drop. We don't want any more dead bodies.'

'And it wouldn't be a good idea to visit Meg's Drop in the dark,' Brenda said. 'It's supposed to be haunted. We already have a witch and evil twins. This case is beginning to sound like one of those spooky horror movies.'

Noel decided to ignore her. 'And what did you find out at the railway station?'

'Like Kevin, not a lot. I waited for the train and spoke to a few of the passengers, but they were all in a hurry to get home on that day, same as they were today. No one remembers seeing Debbie Lansdale. There used to be a camera covering the exit, but it got broken so many times it was taken down. Someone thinks they saw a black four-by-four, but it had two women in it drinking coffee from plastic cups. There's a coffee machine at the station.' She opened her eyes wide. 'Oh, my god! It must have been the identical twins plotting their next move!'

Noel got up from his desk and picked up his jacket. 'Oh, go home, both of you.'

He didn't believe in coincidences. Maybe the woman found in Meg's Drop was just the result of an unfortunate accident. But, then again, maybe not.

★ ★ ★

'Dora added something to her pot on the stove and made a note in a pad she kept on the dresser. Warts,' she said. 'People used to rub them with a frog, but a twig of witch hazel works just as well.'

'I'm glad,' Cass said dryly. She didn't fancy a kitchen full of frogs. 'Can we talk about Debbie?'

Dora turned from the stove and crossed her arms. 'If we must.'

'We couldn't break her alibi. She was definitely at the clinic at the time Michael died.'

'So she says.'

Cass gave a little sigh of exasperation. 'No, Mother. That's what everyone says. The receptionist, the nurse, the consultant. They all say she was there. They saw her on that day and at that time. There was no mistake.'

'Quite obviously there was,' Dora said. She uncrossed her arms and sat down at the table. 'Noel Raven is missing something. I told him that. He's a clever man, not stifled by convention. He'll find what he's looking for eventually, but he needs your help.'

'Why on earth would he need my help? I'm not a detective.'

Dora shook her head. 'I don't know why. But I do know it's going to take both of you to find the answer.' She turned back to the stove and gave her pot another stir. 'Somehow you're joined to him, Cassie. There's a link between you. Without Noel Raven you'll be in grave danger.'

Cass looked at her mother's back. She had a feeling she was in more danger *with* Noel Raven than without him. She remembered that spark of electricity between them, a shock strong enough to knock her out. And he had hardly touched her. She couldn't begin to imagine what would have happened if he got really close — if he kissed her.

Where did that thought come from, for goodness sake? She didn't even like the man and she was quite sure he didn't particularly like her.

'Do you think she might have an accomplice?' she asked her mother. 'That's the only way Debbie could have done it. But what if she didn't do it? What if his death had nothing to do with her? Do you think Michael might have been involved with drugs? Maybe without even knowing? Perhaps some-one used his boat to smuggle stuff and they thought he'd found out about it. That would be enough of a motive for murder.'

Dora turned to look at her daughter, a spoon in her hand. 'Do you think that?'

'No. Oh, I don't know. It's possible,

isn't it? Even though I can't imagine Michael being involved in anything illegal.'

'And I can't imagine him being gullible enough to be taken in by that woman.'

'So? What are we left with?'

'The impossible.'

Dora turned back to her pot just as the telephone started ringing. Cass looked at her mother and then picked up the phone. 'Hello?'

'Hi. Is that Cass? Debbie here. I just wanted to let you know I've arranged the funeral for Monday. I know it's a bit quick — they've only just released Michael's body — but there was a spare slot at the crematorium and I didn't think it was a good idea to drag things out any longer. As you know, Michael was semi-retired, so it will just be family and one or two of his business associates here in England. Is that OK with you and your mother?'

Cass wondered briefly what would happen if she said no, it wasn't OK at all. 'Hang on a minute, Debbie, while I speak to my mother.' She pushed the little button that put the caller on hold and looked at Dora. 'The funeral is at the crematorium on Monday and Debbie wants to know if it's OK with us.' She held out the phone. 'Do you want to talk to her?'

Dora gave Cass a disbelieving look. 'Why would I? Nothing I said would change anything.'

Which was very true. 'Just tell me the time and I'll be there,' she told Debbie. 'Will there be flowers?'

'Yes, of course. I've organised flowers for the chapel and chosen a beautiful polished-oak coffin. You don't have to worry. Michael will have a really lovely send-off.'

The fact that Michael's money was going to pay for his really lovely send-off seemed a bit ironic, but Cass had already learned that Debbie didn't do things by halves. She ended the call and went over to her mother, who was vigorously stirring a pot of twigs. 'There are going to be flowers,' she said gently. 'Do you want me to organise something from us?'

When Dora looked up her eyes were moist. 'He liked roses,' she said. 'But something simple. I'm not going to compete with his wife. I don't need to.'

Cass smiled. 'No, you don't need to. He loved you a lot longer.' She put her arm round her mother's shoulders and gave her a brief hug. 'I'll sort something out.'

She made her way back to her studio and turned on the computer. She needed something special in the way of roses, but something understated. Half an hour later she gave up on the garden centres and tried a well-known local rose grower. She wanted a rose bush in a tub, one that could be planted out later, and chose a standard floribunda in full bloom with a profusion of pure white flowers. It was a beautiful little tree, but it was the name of the rose that decided her. It seemed particularly appropriate.

The rose came in a polished metal tub that she had been assured would stand up to all weathers, so she arranged for it to be sent to the crematorium and included with the other floral tributes before it was moved to the garden of remembrance. She wanted to take a photo of the tree at the funeral to show her mother.

By the time she went to bed that night she was exhausted. The evening meal with her mother had been quiet, with neither of them in the mood for conversation. Michael's funeral should have bought closure, but Cass knew it wouldn't. There was no way Noel was going to solve the case by Monday, and on that day Michael would be gone, with only a rose tree to remember him by.

★　★　★

Monday dawned bright and beautiful, with an azure blue sky and not a cloud in sight. Cass dressed carefully. She

236

didn't think Michael would appreciate an all-black outfit, so she chose a short black dress with tiny white spots and teamed it with a matching wide-brimmed sunhat. She thought long and hard about the shoes, and then slipped her feet into a pair of black patent court shoes with four-inch heels. She topped her outfit off with designer sunglasses from a factory outlet. Now no one would notice if she cried.

Dora studied her thoughtfully. 'You look like a film star in disguise. Are you trying to outdo Michael's wife, by any chance?'

Cass grinned. 'The thought never entered my head. Do you think she'll go with the grieving widow look, or opt for high fashion? She can afford designer everything now, can't she?'

'Michael left us enough to help with the bills, and he provided well for his two children, but his wife got everything else. The boat, both the houses, and his share of the business. He made a new will when he married her.'

Cass sighed. 'I expect he thought he had plenty of time to change his mind if it didn't work out. You must admit it gives her a good motive for pushing him into the pool, even though we know she didn't do it.' Dora made a noise that sounded suspiciously like a hiss, and Cass laughed. 'The cream of Norton's police force has done its best to pin it on her, but it won't stick. I think Noel Raven almost considered an identical twin, but that won't work either.' She hesitated, looking at her mother. 'You do realise we may never know how Michael died.'

Dora pinched her lips together. 'Yes, we will.'

Cass was about to answer when she heard a noise. She cocked her head to one side. 'Was that someone knocking on the front door?' She moved through the hall and opened the door, blinking in the sunlight. Noel stood in front of her in a dark suit, his black hair combed straight back off his face and no stubble on his chin. He looked, she thought, rather magnificent.

He gave her a wry smile. 'I've come to take you to the funeral.'

She had a job not to laugh. 'Your choice of venue for a date leaves a lot to be desired, Mr Raven. First of all a clinic, and now a crematorium.'

He stepped inside and followed her into the kitchen. 'I know your mother can't go, and I didn't want you to go on your own.' He looked at Dora. 'Hello, Dora. I'm sorry you can't come with us.'

'So am I, but I wouldn't get past the gate. Take care of Cassie for me.'

'For goodness sake, Mother. I'm going to a funeral, not into a war zone.' Cass smiled at Noel. 'It will be nice to have some company, though, so thank you.' Having him beside her might stop her bawling her eyes out. She was sure Mrs Lansdale would have herself under tight control.

'And I need to check out any strangers at the funeral,' Noel added, rather spoiling what she'd thought was a nice gesture.

'The killer returning to the scene of the crime?' Dora asked. 'I thought they only did that in books. But you may be right on this occasion.'

'Sometimes they come to watch the final scene of their play. Generally, it's not a good idea. Murderers always think all the evidence gets burned with the body. They forget we've had weeks to collect what we need.'

'We'd better go,' Cass said. She turned to her mother. 'I'll take a photo of the flowers, including our rose tree.' She kissed her mother on the cheek. 'I wish you could come with us, but I know you can't. I'll say goodbye to Michael for both of us.'

* * *

'It's a shame your mother can't leave the house,' Noel said, as he helped Cass into his car. 'Doesn't she ever go outside?'

Cass shook her head. 'She can't breathe. If she goes outside she stops breathing altogether and passes out.

She's been told she could die.'

'What started it off?'

'She got mugged about six months ago. Badly enough to need hospital treatment. She hasn't been outside the house since.'

'But she goes out on to the patio. I've seen her.'

Cass shrugged. 'There's no rhyme or reason to it, it just happens. She says the courtyard is safe, but she can't go any further away from the house.'

'So it's psychological? All in her head?'

'Either that, or what she told me is true and my father put a curse on her.'

Noel turned his head to grin at her. 'I'll go along with the psychological theory for the time being, if that's OK with you.'

'So you think she's mad.'

'Good lord, no.' He looked shocked. 'People with agoraphobia aren't mad. I have a fear of falling, which is very real, believe me. Not vertigo — I don't mind high places; I'm just afraid of falling off

241

them. If someone made me bungee jump I'd probably stop breathing and die, just like your mother. Besides, she had a bad experience. I don't wonder she doesn't feel safe outside. That doesn't make her mad. It's wrong to categorize people.'

Cass smiled. 'How about spells and curses? How do you categorize those?'

'I wouldn't attempt to, but I agree with Shakespeare that there are more things in heaven and earth than we have dreamt of. So, for the moment, taking into account thunderstorms and electric shocks, I'll keep an open mind.'

★ ★ ★

Dora watched Noel's car turn the corner and disappear out of sight. She felt helpless. Something was going to happen to Cassandra, she could feel it in the air, and for the first time in months she felt trapped. She couldn't leave the confines of the house, so she had to trust Noel to take care of her daughter, and she wasn't sure if he was strong enough.

She didn't drink bottled alcohol, but she had a stash of fermented fruit drinks in the kitchen that were quite potent. She picked one of the stronger ones, poured it into a glass, and walked out on to the patio with the drink in her hand. There must be a way through the barrier. Nobody else could feel it, but to her it was a physical thing. An invisible wall that could kill her. The doctor had assured her that the barrier was just the result of physical trauma, and one day it would disappear, but that hadn't happened yet.

She pushed open the gate leading to the lane and took a deep breath. She knew what to expect, but her first step outside was like walking into a vacuum. In that one second she knew just how a landed fish must feel when it hits the deck of a boat. She moved back inside and closed the gate again.

Damn Hector! He had no right to do this to her.

She tried calling Cassandra on her mobile phone, but the call went straight to voicemail. It was as she had expected; no one leaves their phone turned on at a funeral. Deciding she had to do something, even if it meant humiliating herself, she went back inside.

The room where Dora did most of her online work was quite small, but she had managed to keep it feminine as well as functional. Her desk was an antique console table with pretty curved legs and two small drawers. A chintz-covered chair fitted snugly underneath, and a modern laptop sat on the polished surface. One wall of the room was filled with shelves holding apothecary bottles. The bottles were old; some made of a strange green glass and some made of pottery with pictures painted on them. Most of the glass ones held dried leaves and seeds. A mirror in a silver filigree frame reflected the light from the single window and made the room look bigger.

Dora sat at her desk and pulled her

laptop towards her. Hector didn't like her contacting him, not when he was out of the country, and for a moment she considered using Skype and really freaking him out. But she didn't need to see his face. She knew exactly what he looked like. She opened a drawer in her desk and took out a picture of the man she had married. Cassandra's father. His name was Henry Moon, commonly called Harry. She only found out Hector was his birth name when she married him. She could understand why he kept his name a secret. Hector wasn't a good name for a sailor.

Her email was brief. *You have to release me. Cassandra is in danger.*

She knew he'd get back to her. Telling him Cassie was in danger would be enough. Even if he thought she was exaggerating, he would have to check to be sure. He had refused to give her his mobile number, even though she had promised never to call him except in an emergency.

While she waited for an answer to her

email, she stared out of her window at the pretty garden beyond. Being confined to the house hadn't bothered her that much up until now; most of her work was done online. Sometimes she added a little something extra to her recipes, but most of the benefit came from her careful selection of plants and roots.

While she was pouring herself another drink, her computer pinged to let her know she had a new message. She took a sip of a pale pink fizzy concoction made from raspberry leaves and pomegranate seeds, and opened her email account.

Release you from what? And what sort of danger? Be more specific.

How specific did he want her to be?

Michael has been murdered. I believe Cassie is with his killer right now. You have put your daughter in danger with your stupid hex.

Was that specific enough for him? She hit the send key harder than necessary. This was a ridiculous way of contacting anyone, particularly in an emergency.

Why couldn't he just conjure up a typhoon or something, instead of asking so many questions? She'd used the word 'hex' deliberately. Hector swore he had no special powers, but she knew better. He was back online almost immediately and Dora smiled to herself. The 'hex' word had done the trick.

The house is safe, Pandora, so it makes sense to stay inside. I'm in the middle of the Atlantic right now so you'll have to handle this yourself, but Cassandra is strong.

Dora closed her eyes for a moment, and then logged out. The man was about as much help as a knitted bucket, but she knew he loved his daughter. If he reached out he could give her extra strength.

She walked out on to the patio again and watched a lone bird circling above in the stormy sky. Perhaps she could send Noel a sign he might understand. She muttered an old incantation she had learned as a child and watched the bird fly away. Hoping she had done something to keep Cassie safe, she headed back inside the house just as the first drop of rain hit the patio. A flash of lightning lit up the sky and a rumble of thunder followed almost immediately.

If Dora had truly believed in the gods of her ancestors, she would have said they were angry.

12

Noel turned in through the gates of the crematorium and found a parking space in the car park. Cass looked around and saw a small group of people standing to one side of the doors leading into the chapel. Wreaths and sprays of flowers lay on the ground behind them. Emma was examining the wreaths, and Debbie was talking animatedly to a large man in a shiny black suit.

She touched Noel on the arm. 'One of Michael's business associates, I presume. Debbie didn't exactly dress for a funeral, did she? She's wearing the necklace I made, but she doesn't seem particularly distraught, and that looks like a designer dress to me.'

'I wouldn't know. I've never worn one.' He took Cass's arm in a firm grip. 'Come on, you can't stay here in the car park all day. Go over and introduce yourself.'

'As what?' she asked bitterly. 'Although I've known Michael since I was a child, I'm not even family, am I?' She looked over at the group by the door. 'His wife and children are here, and they're real family. I shouldn't have come.'

He kept hold of her arm. 'You're here to represent your mother. She wouldn't chicken out. And look, someone is waving to you.'

Cass saw Liz get out of her car and smiled with delight. She had thought her friend would be working. She raised her hand and gave a small wave back.

Liz caught up with them as they walked across the car park, and Cass saw her give Noel the once-over. She introduced him as they walked slowly towards the group of people.

Before Cass could speak to Emma, Debbie had dragged her balding friend over to meet them. 'Oh, Cassandra, I'm so glad you could come. This is Cassandra Moon, Mr Connaught. The daughter of someone Michael knew a long time ago, before he went to Marbella.'

That just about sums me up, Cass thought. *Someone from Michael's distant past who's come along because she can't resist a good cremation.* She felt a hand on her arm and turned to see Noel standing beside her.

'And I'm the detective inspector who's handling the inquiry into Michael's death,' he told Mr Connaught with a bland smile.

Cass watched Debbie's face turn pink with annoyance as the fat, balding man called Mr Connaught turned sharply to look at Noel. 'I thought Michael had an accident. Fell into the swimming pool, or some such thing.'

'Or some such thing,' Noel repeated. 'I'm sorry, I can't talk about an ongoing case.' He moved away and turned to look at the flower tributes, smiling when he saw the large cross made of arum lilies and gold chrysanthemum heads. It was so over the top only one person could have chosen it. He touched Cass on the arm and pointed to the little tree standing proud and tall amongst the wreaths. 'That's yours, isn't it? From you and Dora.' He picked up the label Cass had left attached to the bush. 'Lover's Folly. How very fitting.'

Liz smiled. 'Under the circumstances I think Michael would have appreciated it.'

Debbie moved up beside them. 'I'm so glad to meet you, Liz. I have so few friends here. Come over for a dip in my pool sometime, Detective. Cass has promised to come back with me today so I won't be all alone. Don't forget, now, Cassie.' She turned her attention back to the flower tributes. 'What a dear little rosebush. I didn't know Michael liked roses.'

'No, you wouldn't, would you,' Cass said pleasantly. She felt Noel's grip on her arm tighten and Liz coughed warningly. They were right. This wasn't the place for sarcasm, although she was sure it was completely lost on Debbie. She hated the way the woman called her Cassie. That diminutive was reserved for her mother and no one else.

'Shall we go inside, ladies?' Noel asked politely.

The service started off quite well, with 'Amazing Grace' sung by a local choir. Cass was glad Noel was beside her. She managed to get away with swallowing a couple of times rather than bursting into tears. The tears were near, but under control. She dare not look at Emma. If Emma cried, Cass knew she would never be able to keep her own emotions in check.

The coffin looked very grand with its gleaming wood and gold fittings, but Cass couldn't imagine Michael choosing it himself. Colin said a few brief words in the way of a eulogy, pointedly leaving out the fact that Michael had recently married the woman sitting in the front row. Cass almost felt sorry for Debbie. What if they had misjudged her and it was shyness that made her seem so cold and unsympathetic? She had been widowed on her honeymoon, and was now living in a place where she knew no one. Michael had left her well off, but all the money in the world wouldn't make up for his untimely death.

Cass came out of her reverie to find they had come to the place in the service where the coffin slides away and the curtains close in front of it. She hated this bit. Michael was about to disappear from their lives forever. There were things she still wanted to say to this man who had been the nearest thing to a father to her. He had been part of her life since she was a little girl, and she was going to miss him dreadfully. Noel seemed to sense how she was feeling. He moved closer and put his hand on her arm. She had trouble resisting the impulse to pull away and wondered what was wrong with her. He was just being kind.

The chapel suddenly felt stifling, the air thick and humid. Sweat broke out on her upper lip and she could feel her skin starting to tingle. She turned her head to look at Noel — and everything went dark.

For a moment she thought she had fainted again, but then she realised all the lights had gone out. It wasn't particularly dark in the chapel, because tall windows high up on the walls let in enough daylight to see by, but there was a lot of confused muttering and shuffling of feet going on. The coffin stayed where it was, in full view of the mourners, and Cass presumed the runners used to slide it behind the curtains were controlled by electricity.

She felt Noel move beside her as he scanned the room. She wondered if he expected another murder to take place in front of him. When her eyes adjusted to the dim light she realised the general atmosphere was one of slight embarrassment. Although it was totally inappropriate, Cass wanted to laugh. This was such an anticlimax it was almost funny. For one horrible moment she imagined everyone in the chapel suddenly breaking into hysterical laugher.

'Another electrical anomaly,' Noel whispered. He had removed his hand from her arm, but the electricity in the room was like a physical thing. The thin material of her dress clung to her thighs, and the tips of her fingers tingled with pins and needles. She shuffled along the seat to get further away from him. The music she hadn't even noticed before had disappeared with the lights, leaving the place eerily quiet. Feet shuffled on the wooden floor, and Emma coughed before looking round apologetically. Cass was just thinking someone should make an announcement about the lack of power, when two brawny men appeared beside the casket and pushed it backwards on its runners. They closed the curtains manually, and a few seconds later the lights flickered and came back on.

Noel reached across and put his hand over hers. 'You OK?'

She moved closer to him. The electricity had gone from the air. 'I am now. It was a bit touch and go there for a minute or two. I was afraid we were both going to disappear in a shower of sparks.'

'That would have livened up the proceedings.' He got to his feet and helped her up. 'I've got a text message from the police station.' He held up his phone. 'I don't know what it's about, but they want me back there.'

'Is it something serious?'

'I don't know yet. Kevin didn't say, just suggested I get back as soon as possible.' Noel dropped the phone in his pocket. 'I'll run you home first.'

Cass shook her head. 'No need. I promised Debbie I'd go back to the house with her so she won't be on her own. She can take me home later, or I'll grab a cab.'

'I don't think it's a good idea to go back to that woman's house.' He looked at her worriedly. 'Just because her alibi checked out . . . '

'I appreciate your concern, Noel, but it's broad daylight and I'm all grown up. I don't need a bodyguard. I've got my phone in my pocket, and if I'm at all worried I'll give you a buzz.'

'I'm not joking, Cass.'

She looked into his eyes and realised he was genuinely worried about her. 'I know you're not.' Without really thinking she stood on tiptoe and planted a kiss on his cheek. 'Thank you for caring about me.'

He looked startled for a moment, and then he grinned. 'No electric sparks? I must be losing my charm.' Before she could stop him he gently brushed his lips over hers. 'That's more like it. I definitely felt something that time.'

He wasn't the only one, she thought, as she watched him walk away. Not anything electrical, but something completely different.

As Noel strode away across the car park Cass touched her lips with the tips of her fingers. That had been totally unexpected. Not that it was a proper kiss. He was just worried about her because if anything happened to her he would feel responsible. She couldn't imagine what could happen to her while she was having a cup of tea with Debbie, but she could always swap cups just to be on the safe side. Forewarned is forearmed, or something like that.

Liz appeared beside her. 'Nice. No wonder you've kept him hidden.' She looked at Cass with a little gleam in her eye. 'Did he just kiss you goodbye?'

'No, of course he didn't. He told me to watch out because I'm going back with Debbie for a cup of tea. He still doesn't trust her.'

'It looked like a kiss to me.'

'Oh, for goodness sake, Liz. It wasn't a kiss, so forget it. There is nothing between Noel Raven and myself. Nothing at all.'

Apart from a few sparks, she thought.

She walked with Liz to her car and watched her friend drive away. As she headed back towards the chapel she could see Debbie talking to the businessman again. Surely she couldn't be interested in a fat, bald guy in a shiny suit? But there was no accounting for taste. Perhaps he was another millionaire and she was collecting them like trophies, killing one before she went on to the next.

Cass wanted to make sure the rose tree went to the garden of remembrance, rather than off to a hospice with the other flowers, but she'd only gone a few yards when Emma waylaid her.

'Cass, do you want us to give you a lift home? I saw the policeman drive off, so you haven't got transport back, have you?'

'No, I'm fine. I promised Debbie I'd go back with her. She'll run me home. I know she'd like you to stay as well, but I expect you want to get off as quickly as possible, don't you?'

Emma nodded. 'We've got our cases in the car. Colin wanted to get away as soon as the service finished.'

Debbie arrived beside them looking a little flushed. 'You are coming back to the house, aren't you, Cass? You promised me.' Her breath caught as she looked around. 'Everyone else seems to be going, and I don't want to be alone just yet.' She looked at Emma. 'You're off as well then, are you?'

Emma nodded guiltily. 'We've got a

long drive home. Thank you for having us. I'm sorry it was in such dreadful circumstances. We must keep in touch.'

'Of course,' Debbie said without much enthusiasm. 'Drive carefully.'

Cass gave Emma a hug. 'Say goodbye to Colin for me. I'll phone you tomorrow.' She was going to miss them both. She walked beside Debbie to the big black car. It was parked in a disabled parking space. 'Are you going to get a new car? Michael always liked enormous cars, but something smaller would be easier to drive — and to park.'

Debbie shrugged. 'A big car like this has its uses.'

She swung herself effortlessly up into the driver's seat and smiled as Cass made a pig's ear of climbing into the car. The step up was quite high and Cass was wearing heels. There was obviously a knack of some sort which she hadn't yet mastered, but as her Mini required a step down rather than up, there was no immediate hurry. She found the lever to move the seat forward and buckled herself in. Debbie seemed in a strange sort of mood, but Cass reminded herself again that the woman had just cremated her husband. That was probably enough to put anyone in a strange mood.

Debbie drove fast but skilfully, and it only took them ten minutes to get back to the house. She parked outside the front door and stepped down from the car, taking a key out of her bag.

'Michael never locked the front door, but I always do. Someone must have come in that day and killed him. The side gate was unlocked, did you know that?'

'Yes. I found him, remember? The gate was unlocked when I got here. I thought that was a bit strange at the time, because Michael was quite security-conscious. Perhaps he knew the person who killed him and let them in himself.' She looked at Debbie. 'Or he drank too much wine and fell into the pool.'

As Debbie headed for the front door, Cass slid down from the car and almost landed in an unladylike heap on the gravel drive. She clutched the back of the seat for support and it shot back on its runners, almost tipping her over again. She fervently hoped Debbie wasn't watching. She was about to pull the seat back into place again when she noticed something shining on the floor. As she bent down for a closer look she saw it was a small silver locket. She picked it up, slammed the car door, and followed Debbie into the house.

Debbie led Cass through into the living area and opened the doors on to the terrace. The storm had passed and the sun was out again, turning the water in the pool to an impossible blue. Steam rose from the damp granite slabs on the terrace and the petals of the roses glittered with a few remaining drops of rain. Cass thought it looked a bit like a film set. Definitely not real.

As Debbie turned round Cass put the locket down on the coffee table. 'I found this in the car.'

Debbie stared at the locket for a

second or two. 'Where did you say you found it?'

'In the car,' Cass repeated. 'Under the passenger seat. When I got out of the car the seat slid back and the locket was on the floor. Michael bought it for you, didn't he?'

For a moment Debbie looked as if she didn't understand the question. 'What?'

Cass frowned. 'The locket. I assume it's yours as it was under the passenger seat.' Debbie looked completely disorientated and Cass wondered if the stress of the funeral was catching up with her.

'Yes,' she said at last. 'Yes, Michael bought it for me. I lost it. In the car.' She stared at Cass for a minute, and then shook her head as if she had just woken up. 'I'm being a bad host. Let me get you a drink.' As Cass went to say something, she held up her hand. 'We both need a drink. I'll just have half a glass of wine and then I can drive you home. Excuse me a minute, the glasses are in the kitchen.'

Cass waited until Debbie had left the room and then she picked up the locket. She remembered Michael emailing her about buying Debbie a silver locket. He had cut their faces out of snapshots and put them inside, 'Just so she doesn't ever forget me,' he had joked. Surely Debbie wouldn't mind if she looked at the photos. She found a little catch and the locket popped open. Cass stared at the pictures inside for a moment, and then she closed the locket and put it back on the table.

The locket was the last piece of the puzzle. Now everything made sense, and she needed to get in touch with Noel Raven urgently. More importantly, she needed to get out of the house. She rummaged in her bag for her phone, and then remembered she had turned it off and dropped it in her pocket at the funeral. She started towards the open doors to the terrace, but at that moment Debbie came back into the room carrying two glasses and a bottle of champagne.

'Sorry about the glasses. I've already broken one of the best crystal ones, so I'm using the second-best from the kitchen.'

Cass had heard about thinking on your feet, but now she was on her feet every thought had left her head. *Don't panic,* she told herself. *You have a phone in your pocket, and all the doors are open. No one is keeping you prisoner.*

13

Debbie set the glasses down on a low table beside the fireplace and took a bottle opener from a drawer in the wall unit. Cass watched her peel the foil from the bottle and remove the metal cage. When she twisted the top, the cork came out with a satisfying pop. She poured the golden liquid into both glasses, but didn't immediately hand one to Cass. Instead, she looked at the locket on the coffee table.

'You looked inside the locket while I was out of the room, didn't you?'

Cass took a breath. It would be useless to lie. She was sure Debbie had memorised the exact position of the locket when she left the room. She had put the bait on the table and, like a fool, Cass had taken it.

'Yes.'

Debbie picked up both glasses of

Champagne and handed one to Cass. She smiled when Cass hesitated. 'Don't worry, it was a new bottle. You saw me open it, heard the cork pop.' She glanced at the bag Cass had been rooting through. 'Were you looking for your phone? I think it would be best to leave it where it is for the moment, don't you?'

Cass wasn't going tell the woman the phone wasn't in her bag. Instead, she said, 'You're not Debbie Lansdale, are you?'

'Goodness me, what a clever girl you are.'

'Why are you pretending to be her?'

Debbie took a sip of her drink and laughed. 'I'm surprised you need to ask me that. Debbie Lansdale was a nobody. A silly little barmaid who giggled her way through life. She had no ambition, no goals, nothing to look forward to except more of the same. Then she met Michael and told him she loved him — and he gave her everything. That shouldn't happen to someone like her.

She was incapable of appreciating any of it. He gave her this beautiful house, and she bought pink cushions and a picture of a Spanish bullfighter to put on the wall. She had no taste at all. I appreciate nice things. I shall soon be a member of the golf club, and I've asked Mr Connaught for a seat on the board of Michael's company. I don't have to worry about the way I speak, or which knife to use in a restaurant.' She smiled. 'I can even open a bottle of Champagne. I belong here, Cassie — surely you can see that.' She poured more wine into her glass. 'Finish your drink; we've a whole bottle to get through, and I want to tell you how clever I've been.'

Cass noticed the picture and the cushions were no longer around, but then, neither was Debbie. She finished the Champagne in her glass and decided she still preferred red wine. She wouldn't have any more to drink because she needed to keep a clear head. She didn't intend to die in this room.

'Who are you?' she asked.

Debbie arched an eyebrow. 'Why, Debbie Lansdale, of course.' Her laugh was a little snigger of glee. 'Once I was called Linda Crow, and I had a boring job in London. I went out to Marbella to find a millionaire, and I actually found him, but the stupid man preferred a little blond barmaid. He said it was because she made him laugh.' Debbie held up the Champagne bottle, but Cass shook her head. 'I could have given him so much more than she did, but I prefer it this way. I have everything I want without having to keep a boring old man happy. I was best friends with them both, you know. When Debbie told me she was getting married I said how pleased I was for her. I was maid of honour at her wedding. She actually asked me to come to England and stay with them in their new house. When I turned up unexpectedly, Michael was really pleased to see me. We had a glass of wine together by the pool. I'd already drugged his wine, but I couldn't wait for him to fall asleep, so I put a cushion over his face. He was heavier than I thought, but I managed to drag him into the pool, and then I took his car and went to pick up his darling wife from the train station.' The woman sitting in front of Cass gurgled with laughter. 'She was pleased to see me, too.'

Cass wondered what had happened to the real Debbie, but she didn't want to know the answer.

'Can I have a glass of water, please?' She was feeling light-headed, probably because she hadn't had any lunch, but she could hardly ask for a sandwich.

Linda leaned across the coffee table and smiled into Cass's eyes. 'Don't you feel very well, dear? My goodness, I didn't think the drug I gave you would take effect this quickly. We'd better get you out to the car while you can still walk.'

Cass tried to concentrate. Drugged? How could she have been drugged? 'I saw you open the bottle. You couldn't have put anything in it.' She vaguely remembered reading about a syringe needle going through a cork into a bottle, but the Champagne bottle had foil round the neck and a cage over the cork.

'No, you're quite right. I didn't put anything in the bottle. It was sleight of hand, like a magic trick. While you were concentrating on the bottle, you didn't look at the glass until it was too late. The stuff was already in your glass when I poured in the Champagne. It just needed a couple of seconds to dissolve.' She frowned at Cass, who had slumped down in her chair. 'You really need to get on your feet, dear. Shall I help you up?'

Cass decided if the woman called her 'dear' one more time, she would kill her. She had no idea how she was going to accomplish the killing, but she would figure it out somehow. She still had a phone in her pocket. If she could stay awake long enough she could call her mother. Dora would know what to do.

Cass staggered as she tried to get to

her feet. She didn't feel too bad at the moment, but she had to pretend she was a lot worse than she was, so she leant more heavily on the woman than she needed to. She didn't want to get in the car, but if she didn't Linda would just wait for her to go to sleep and drag her there. She certainly hadn't got enough strength left for a fight.

Linda helped her into the car but didn't do up the seat belt. Cass stored that information away for later. When the car stopped she might be able to make a run for it. It wasn't until they were on their way that she thought to wonder where they were going. She was having trouble fighting the urge to sleep, but she knew she daren't close her eyes even for a second. It was the same as wanting to close your eyes when you're driving a car. However tired you are, you can't risk it.

She managed to get her phone out of her pocket and hold it in her hand, but that was as far as she got. All she had to do was turn the phone on, press the letter D and then the dial button, and her mother would answer. But when she ran a finger over the buttons she realised she had no idea where the letter D actually was. If she turned the phone on and held it up in front of her face, it was going to look a bit obvious. Besides, if she got through to her mother and didn't speak, Dora would start shouting down the phone and Linda would hear.

How do they do it in the movies? she wondered.

She lolled her head and pretended she was asleep while she studied the scenery outside the window. Linda had kept to the side roads, so opening the door and falling out of the car wasn't an option. She would either get run over, or Linda would stop the car and put a cushion over her face.

Five minutes later she knew exactly where they were heading and didn't like it one little bit. She tried to work out a plan of action, but her eyelids felt so heavy they were starting to close of their own volition. Any minute now they would get to Meg's Drop and Linda would toss her over the edge.

A few minutes later she heard the woman swear under her breath, and then the car stopped with a screech of brakes. Linda undid her seat belt and leant towards Cass. She had her hand at her neck, pulling on the necklace. Cass thought how pretty the ruby looked in the sunshine; it was glowing with an inner fire.

'I can't undo this damned thing. Can you get it off me?'

Cass blinked. 'Why do you want it off?'

'Don't ask stupid questions. Just take it off.'

Cass blinked again, and then shook her head. She was quite sure she no longer had the co-ordination needed to undo a small gold clasp on a chain round someone's neck. And why should she? 'If you wanted me to do something like that you shouldn't have drugged me. My head feels fuzzy and my fingers feel like sausages.' She heard herself say sausages like someone on their fourth bottle of vodka.

Linda pushed a button to drop the window a couple of inches. 'That'll keep you awake a bit longer. She pulled at the gold chain again. 'I want this thing off.'

Cass giggled, and wiggled her fat, dead fingers. 'Hard luck.'

She felt the slap round her face, but it didn't really hurt, and she wondered what Linda had dosed her with. Some sort of anaesthetic, probably. She even managed a smile. Now what? However many slaps Linda gave her, her fingers still wouldn't work enough to undo the clasp on the necklace.

Linda started the car and pulled back out onto the road. She had one hand on the steering wheel and the other holding the pendant away from her skin. Cass saw her pull on the chain a couple of times, but it didn't break, which was surprising, because with the way it was being tugged it should have done.

Meg's Drop was at the top of a hill. Not a very steep hill, but at some point in time one side of the hill had crumbled away, leaving a sheer drop of about fifty feet. The sides were dotted with large outcrops of rock and scrubby bushes, and there was still the wreck of a car at the bottom. Some boys had thought it would be fun to push it over the edge. The drop had never been considered a particularly dangerous place. There had been a couple of accidental falls over the years, but no suicides, because death wasn't a foregone conclusion — and that was what Cass was banking on. She had read somewhere that you were more likely to survive a fall if you were unconscious. Besides, it would definitely be less painful. She could see bollards and yellow tape and wondered what they were doing there. Linda must have seen them too, because she cursed loudly and swung the car in a wide loop.

'Damn! They shouldn't have found her yet. We'll have to go further along.'

Cass saw her tug at the locket again. 'They won't be able to identify her. No one will. She's a nobody.'

Before she lost the use of her hands completely, Cass reached up and pushed her phone out through the gap in the window. It might not be much use as a communications device, but it might work as a clue — proof that she'd been there.

Linda drove the car into the trees and picked up a trail that came out further along the drop. By the time Linda stopped the car, Cass was having trouble hanging on to any sort of awareness. When the door opened beside her without any warning, she fell out onto the grass. Seat belt not done up, she reminded herself. Although she had fallen on her face, she could see the rim of the ravine out of one eye, and knew it would only take a gentle push to send her over the edge — but the grass felt so nice against her cheek. All soft and comfortable. She was just thinking it would be a good place to go to sleep, when Linda caught hold of her ankles and started to pull.

Cass dug her fingers into the grass, but she was still moving inexorably towards the edge. In a last-ditch effort, she summoned up all her remaining strength and swung her legs round in a convulsive movement that caught Linda on the backs of her knees. The woman went down with a thud, but was back on her feet in seconds, absolutely furious. She kicked Cass hard.

'That'll teach you to mess with me, you little bitch.'

Cass felt the pain that time. She tried to curl her body into a ball, waiting for the next kick, but none of her muscles seemed to be working properly. She knew she was very near the edge of the drop. One more kick would send her down amongst the rocks. If she had inherited any witchery talents, she really needed them now. Power over gemstones, her mother had said, but what good would that do her? The only gemstone was the ruby hanging round

Linda's neck, sitting so prettily against her bare skin. A ruby with a fire inside it — hot as a furnace.

The second kick never came. Linda screamed — the sound echoing along the chasm below — and Cass smiled as the darkness overwhelmed her.

14

Noel drove back to the police station wishing he hadn't left Cass behind. He could feel bad vibes. Dora was right — something terrible was going to happen.

He jumped like a scared rabbit when a black shape thudded against the windscreen. He slowed the car so he could look behind him, and saw what had caused the noise straight away. There was a bird lying in the middle of the road. Worried it might not be dead, he stopped on the grass verge and got out. It was a large black bird, something like a crow, but it was quite dead. He moved the limp body to the side of the road, surprised at the weight of it, and drove on to the police station, wondering why he still felt so unsettled.

Brenda and Kevin were waiting for him in his office. 'Wow! You look good,'

Brenda said with something like awe in her voice. 'It obviously takes a funeral to bring out the best in some people.'

'New suit?' Kevin asked, fingering the lapel of Noel's jacket.

'Get your hands off me,' Noel growled. He took off his jacket and threw it over the back of his chair. 'I came straight here because you texted me at the funeral. What have you got for me?'

'How did the funeral go?' Brenda asked. 'Is Cassandra Moon OK?'

'Yeah, fine.' He flopped into his chair and eased his feet out of his shoes. 'All the lights went out in the middle of the service, and I killed a bird on the way back here, but other than that it was pretty normal.' He looked at Brenda expectantly. 'So?'

'We may have an ID on the latest body,' she said.

'What do you mean, you may have?'

Kevin looked uncomfortable. 'We thought we had, but we'd only got dental records to go on, so it's not conclusive. I've faxed a photo of the victim to the Spanish police to get a positive ID.'

'It was Kevin who thought to check for dental records with the Spanish authorities,' Brenda said. 'It just seemed too much of a coincidence, another body so soon.'

Noel stared at them. 'You'd better start talking sense, and that goes for both of you, because at the moment I have no idea what either of you are talking about.'

Kevin fidgeted. 'I didn't think you'd be back so soon. I'd rather have confirmation before I say any more. I might be wrong.'

Noel rolled his eyes. He was tired and he didn't want riddles, he wanted answers. 'Why don't you tell me what you think you might be wrong about? Then I'll tell you whether you are wrong.' He looked across the room to where Brenda was trying to look invisible. 'Do you think he's wrong, Brenda?'

She shook her head. 'You said we had to think outside the box, so we did. The answer we got seemed impossible, but now we've had time to think about it, it makes sense.'

'If you don't tell me what you found out I'm going to bash your damned heads together. Who is the dead woman?'

'Debbie Lansdale.'

Noel closed his eyes. He needed a moment to think. When you have eliminated the impossible, whatever remains . . . He could almost feel the pieces of the puzzle clicking together in his head. He got to his feet and walked over to his murder board.

'So we've got an impostor. Do we know who she is?'

'Not yet. But she must have already known a lot about the Lansdales, like where they were both going to be at a particular time. She knew Debbie Lansdale was going to be in London all day. That was what gave her an unbreakable alibi.'

'Two women were seen sitting in a big black car at the station.' Noel moved a card on his board. 'The impostor took a taxi from the station to the house, killed Michael Lansdale, and then drove to the station in his car. If Debbie knew her husband was going to pick her up, she would have been looking out for the car. Pleased to see it. So the impostor killed Debbie — or at least drugged her, dumped the body in Meg's Drop, and then drove back to the house. That accounts for the discrepancy in the timeline.'

'What excuse would she give for turning up in Mr Lansdale's car?'

'Probably said he wasn't feeling well, so he asked her to pick his wife up from the station.'

'She's a good actress,' Brenda said. 'The hysterics when she arrived at the murder scene were pretty convincing.'

'She took me in,' Noel agreed. He wasn't going to admit some of his attention might have been taken up with Cass. He suddenly remembered she had said she was going back with Debbie for a cup of tea. Not a good idea under the circumstances. But it was just a quick cup of tea. The woman wasn't going to kill Cass in broad daylight — she had no reason to.

'What was her motive?' Brenda asked curiously. 'Money? She's pretty well off now, isn't she?'

Noel shook his head. 'I don't think it's just the money. I've met the woman. She wants the lifestyle that goes with it. She's a sociopath. She has no morals. As far as she's concerned she's entitled to the good life, and it was there for the taking.'

Brenda shuddered. 'Anything that got in her way she removed, like swatting a fly. I was on her side at the beginning, feeling sorry for her. I didn't believe she was a killer.'

Noel shuffled cards on his board, getting them in the right order. Had they got enough to bring her in? He doubted it. Most of the evidence was circumstantial. They were going to have to wait for confirmation on the dental records before they had anything concrete. He stared at his board. So what would the woman do next? Lansdale's body was in the ground now, and supposedly the impostor didn't know they'd found Debbie's body, so she'd be feeling safe. She had no reason to hurt Cassandra.

His phone rang, and he pulled it out of his pocket impatiently. 'Yes?'

'Noel? Cassie's in trouble.'

'How do you know she's in trouble, Dora?' He felt his heart lose a beat. 'What happened?'

'I trusted you, Noel. You should have brought her home. I sent you a sign, but it was too late. You have to find her.'

'She's gone back for a cup of tea with Debbie,' he said, trying to calm himself down as much as Dora. 'I'm sure she's fine.'

'No, she isn't. She's not answering her phone. She's in terrible danger, Noel. Please find her.'

He muttered a few more comforting words and stuffed the phone back in his pocket. 'We have to go to the Lansdale house. I think Cass is in trouble.' He grabbed his jacket, wishing he had a gun. 'We'll think of a reason for our visit when we get there.'

He thought about using the blue light, but decided it might do more harm than good. He had no idea why he was racing through the country lanes like a demented idiot on the advice of a witch, but he believed every word Dora had said. Cass was in terrible danger.

'Her car's not here,' Brenda said worriedly as Noel screeched to a halt outside the house.

He flung open the door. 'She didn't have her car. I drove her to the funeral and Debbie — or whatever her name is — drove Cass back here. Is the Lansdales' car in the garage?'

Kevin pushed at the door to the double garage. 'Don't know. The door's electronic. You need a remote.'

'Try the back entrance to the house. If they left in a hurry she might have forgotten to lock up.'

'You're going to break in?' Brenda asked apprehensively.

'If the back doors are open, I won't have to, will I?'

Noel followed Kevin through the gate to the back of the house with Brenda only a few feet behind. Kevin had already pushed back the sliding doors and gone inside. The three of them went from room to room like a police raid on TV. Noel was feeling both frantic and foolish at the same time. What if Cass had decided to walk home, or gone somewhere else entirely? The whole situation was unreal; a fantasy with witches and ravens and deadly potions all jostling for position. He stood inside the Lansdales' designer kitchen trying to decide what to do next. There was no need to look inside the garage. He was pretty sure Debbie had gone, and taken Cass with her.

Brenda called from the living area. 'You need to see this.'

As Noel hurried back to the lounge, Kevin clattered down the stairs from above. They arrived together to find Brenda holding an open locket on the palm of her hand. 'It was on the coffee table. Open, like this.'

Noel took it from her. 'That's the wife, the real Mrs Lansdale, and her husband. If we get a dental match back from Spain, this is all the evidence we need.' He closed the locket and dropped it in his pocket. 'But first we have to find Cassandra Moon. Her mother was right — if she's with the impostor, she really is in danger.'

'Meg's Drop,' Brenda said. 'It worked for the woman the first time.'

Noel was already heading for his car, trying not to run. He never panicked. That was why he had been promoted. He always had a cool head in an emergency, a detachment that was perfect for police work. So why was his heart trying to climb up into his throat, and why did he want so desperately to break into a run?

Kevin had to make a leap for it, but he managed to scramble into the back of the car as it headed out through the gates. All Noel could think about was Cass at the bottom of Meg's Drop, her face and body mangled so badly no one could identify her. But as he gripped the steering wheel he felt a tiny spark of electricity, a tingle against the palm of his hand, and knew she was still alive.

'We have to get to her quickly. She doesn't have much strength left.'

Brenda didn't question him. 'Do you want me to phone for an ambulance?'

'We can't call an ambulance until we know where she is,' Kevin said from the back of the car. 'It will just waste time in the long run. And if she's at the bottom of Meg's Drop, we have to get her up first.'

'Yeah, you're right. No point in getting ahead of ourselves.' Noel let go of the steering wheel with one hand and flexed his fingers, forcing himself to slow down. If he wrecked the car now, no one would find Cass. 'Radio in,' he told Brenda. 'Let them know where we're going. Another car at the scene might be a good idea.'

'The woman must know she's going to get caught in the end.'

'No, she doesn't. That's just the point. She thinks she's too clever for the average person to ever find her out. And you must admit she's done a pretty good job so far.'

Brenda turned her head to look at him. 'Surely she doesn't believe she can go on killing people willy-nilly? If we don't find Cassandra Moon, everyone will be out hunting for her and she'll be found in the end, even if she's at the bottom of Meg's Drop.'

'But you still need evidence to pin anything on the killer. There was no match for Debbie Lansdale's dental records in England because she'd never had any work done over here. And we might never have found out the identity of the woman at the bottom of Meg's Drop, because we were looking in the wrong place. Smoke and mirrors, misdirection, sleight of hand. Call it what you like, it very nearly worked.'

If sleight of hand came up against magic, he wondered which one would win. He had a vision of Dora and Cass standing side by side with lightning flashing in the distance, and he knew where he'd put his money.

'We still need proof,' Brenda said quietly, as Noel swung to a stop on the grass at the top of the hill. 'There's nothing here.'

Noel closed his eyes in defeat. He'd forgotten about the bollards and streamers of yellow crime-scene tape. It was a dead giveaway. It shouted from the housetops that the body had been found — and possibly identified. The killer would be long gone by now, and Cass with her.

Disappointment hit him like a blow to the heart. He'd been so sure. So positive Cass would be here and that she would still be alive. So positive that this was the right place.

He swung open the car door and got out, almost afraid to look down into the drop. He gingerly walked to the very edge, where he could see the bushes and rubble that hid the bottom. Anything could be down there. Half a dozen cars and an assortment of bodies. A whole Boy Scout pack. It was pure luck that Debbie Lansdale had been found at all.

'Someone was here recently,' Kevin called out from over near the trees. 'There are tyre marks where a car swung round. It must have been on full lock because it's dug up the soil.'

Noel walked over and peered down at the grooves in the grass, and then followed them for a short distance. The ground was very dry after the long spell of good weather, so the car must have been moving at quite a speed. 'No point following the tracks; they run out a bit further on.'

'Try her phone,' Brenda suggested. 'She might answer this time.'

Without much hope, Noel pushed the buttons.

'Beethoven's Fifth,' Brenda said, looking round. 'Where's it coming from?'

'It's hers.' Noel was already on the

move. 'Cass's mobile phone. She must have dropped it.'

'Beethoven's Fifth,' Kevin said in a puzzled voice. 'That's a strange one.'

The phone was lit up like a little beacon, half-hidden in long grass near the trees. Noel picked it up. 'So we know the Debbie woman was here, but that doesn't help us find out where she's gone. If she's got any sense she'll be miles away by now.'

'But she thinks she's invincible,' Brenda said, 'so I don't think she will have gone far.'

A flock of crows had been screeching at one another in the tops of the trees, but now they stopped all at once, as if someone had smothered the sound with a blanket. Noel looked up and saw the birds still flapping around, but silently.

The scream cut through the silence like a scalpel on glass. A scream of pain — a long, drawn-out wail that made his skin crawl. The birds took off in a panic, their wings making the air move as they left the trees in a noisy black cloud.

He started running for his car, not looking to see whether Brenda and Kevin were following. Once they were on board, he swung the car round and headed into the trees, finding the track more by luck than judgement, the sound of the scream still echoing in his ears.

The first thing he saw when the car broke from the trees was Cass, lying as still as death at the edge of the drop. He was already running towards her still body before he noticed the woman kneeling on the ground clutching her neck. He ignored the gasping noises the woman was making, and dropped to his knees beside Cass. She looked scarily pale and far too still. He reached for her wrist to try and find a pulse, but Brenda was there before him. She put the tips of her fingers on Cass's neck and shook her head.

'I can't feel anything.'

Noel pushed her roughly aside. 'She's not dead.'

Trying to remember what he'd learned about CPR, he pressed the heel of his hand in the middle of Cass's chest. As soon as he touched her, her body convulsed, arching upward so only her head and heels were touching the ground. He felt the blast of electricity right down to his toes, and his brain bounced inside his skull. He wondered for a moment if either of them could survive such a massive shock, but Cass's eyes flew open and she gasped for air like a landed fish. Brenda helped her sit up so she could breathe more easily.

'I've been drugged,' she said, her speech still slightly slurred. 'And that woman is not Debbie.'

'I know,' Noel said. 'She's an impostor.' He wanted to touch Cass. More than anything, he wanted to hold her in his arms, but something had just happened that was more than weird, and he could still feel ripples beneath his skin. He had a feeling if he touched Cass too soon he might kill her. 'Look after her,' he told Brenda.

Kevin was bending down beside the impostor. He looked up when Noel approached. 'She's been burned. Got a big burn mark on her neck. Third-degree, I reckon. Must've hurt like hell. It was her that screamed.'

'And brought us all here in time to rescue Cass. A bit ironic, that, when you come to think about it.'

'She OK? Cassandra?'

Noel nodded. 'I think she'll be fine. She's been drugged, and this sad creature was going to push her over the edge of Meg's Drop.' He bent down and stared at the raw red weal on the woman's neck. It looked charred round the edges. 'How did she say this happened?'

'The ruby necklace. Says it got hot enough to burn a hole in her neck.' He held out his hand, the ruby gleaming serenely in the centre of his palm. 'I took the necklace off her, but it's not hot. Not even warm.'

'We all know the woman's mad. She smokes like a chimney, so she probably dropped a lighted cigarette on herself. But no one is going to believe anything she says, anyway.'

He stood up as a police car bumped over the grass towards them, closely followed by a first-response car with two paramedics on board. 'I want that woman in a cell, not a hospital bed. Get the paramedics to patch her up and then send her off in the police car. I'll take Cassandra home. She doesn't need a hospital. Her mother can look after her better than anyone else.'

Once more, Dora was at the front door when he drove up. She held out her arms to Cass, who staggered into them. Noel followed the two women into the kitchen.

Dora was dressed in her usual floral caftan, her pale hair a shimmering halo, but her eyes looked tired and Noel thought he could see new lines on her pretty face. She helped Cass to a chair and then handed her a tall glass of something thick and brown.

'I have to get the drugs out of your

system, Cassie, so drink this. It tastes foul, and it might make you sick, but you'll be feeling fine by tomorrow.' She looked at Noel. 'Thank you. You saved her life.'

'I don't know what happened out there.'

Dora smiled. 'You don't need to. In the end everything worked out the way it was supposed to. We were all too late to save Michael, but you got there in time to save Cassie.'

Noel knew there would be a mountain of paperwork waiting for him, but he needed the answers to a couple of questions. 'On the phone, you said something about sending me a sign.'

Dora gave him an innocent look. 'Did I? I was in a panic. I don't remember what I said.'

'Nothing to do with a big black bird, then? A big dead bird that looked like a raven.'

Dora smiled. 'You weren't supposed to kill it. It would have guided you to Cassie.'

'Sorry. Next time one flies straight into my windscreen, I'll try to remember that.'

Cass scowled at him from her chair. 'You're talking rubbish like my mother, Noel, and I can only deal with one rubbish-talker at a time.'

'I'd better go, then. I'll call in tomorrow to make sure you're both OK.' He took her hand. 'I know you don't want to answer questions right now, but how did that ruby get hot enough to leave a burn mark?'

Cass gave him a weak smile. 'I have no idea, Noel. I'm going to give the necklace to Emma. It will be safe with her.' She yawned. 'I'd ask you to stay for dinner, but as I'm really tired and quite likely to throw up, it probably isn't a good idea.'

Dora walked with him to the front door. 'Thank you again, Noel, for saving my daughter's life.'

He smiled as he bent to kiss her cheek. 'I think you know more about that than I do, but we found Michael

Lansdale's murderer, so it's all over.'

'I don't think it's over. Not yet.'

'Probably not. There will always be evil around. But I can't save the world on my own, Dora.'

'You won't have to,' she said. 'Cass will be there to help you.'

THE END

We do hope that you have enjoyed reading this large print book.

Did you know that all of our titles are available for purchase?

We publish a wide range of high quality large print books including:
Romances, Mysteries, Classics
General Fiction
Non Fiction and Westerns

Special interest titles available in large print are:
The Little Oxford Dictionary
Music Book, Song Book
Hymn Book, Service Book

Also available from us courtesy of Oxford University Press:
Young Readers' Dictionary
(large print edition)
Young Readers' Thesaurus
(large print edition)

For further information or a free brochure, please contact us at:
Ulverscroft Large Print Books Ltd.,
The Green, Bradgate Road, Anstey,
Leicester, LE7 7FU, England.
Tel: (00 44) **0116 236 4325**
Fax: (00 44) **0116 234 0205**

Other titles in the
Linford Romance Library:

MYSTERY AT CASA LARGO

Miranda Barnes

When Samantha Davis is made redundant, she turns to her boyfriend Steve for consolation — only to discover he is cheating on her. With both job and relationship having vanished in the space of one day, she feels left on the scrapheap, until her mother suggests she travel to Portugal to work at her friend Georgina's guesthouse. There, she meets Georgina's attractive son, Hugo — and the mysterious, taciturn Simon . . .

TAKE ME, I'M YOURS

Gael Morrison

Melissa D'Angelo is tired of being the only twenty-four-year-old virgin in Seattle. Before entering medical school, she needs a lover with no strings attached. Harvard Law School graduate Jake Mallory loves women and they love him. But a pregnancy scare with a woman he barely knew birthed a vow of celibacy and a growing need for love, family and commitment. The moment Jake and Melissa meet at a local club, passion ignites. But Melissa can't allow sex to lead to love — and love and family are all Jake wants . . .

BABY ON LOAN

Liz Fielding

Jessie is temporarily caring for her adorable baby nephew when she gets evicted from her apartment! She has no choice but to let Patrick Dalton think she's a single mother, so that he'll let her stay with him. The last thing he wants is Jessie and her baby bringing chaos to his serene home — but in no time his life is filled with laughter and the very beautiful Jessie. Until he discovers that his growing love for his houseguests is based on a lie . . .